sepia

If only he hadn't. If only she had.

Herlinde Cayzer

herlindesnippets.blogspot.com

Praise for *sepia*

'I thoroughly enjoyed reading your novel *sepia*. I believe its message to be honest and uplifting, while reminding us of the nightmare of the Nazi era which should never be forgotten. The novel is also a reminder of the power of the human spirit to overcome trauma of the past, hence moving on to a positive future. This is a good story that needs to be told.'
Gary Crew, Emeritus Professor, Creative Writing

'It's a well-thought-out story with everything coming full circle with a surprise ending. I like how you portrayed the two boys as unwilling participants and the different stance each took in a time both unfair and cruel.'
Donna Munro, Author

'A beautifully written and moving story, intertwining memories and dreams, loss and happiness and revealing the strength of human courage and survival. Shifting perspective between the past and present, the author creates a world filled with surprise, humour, heartache and ultimately redemption. A thoroughly enjoyable story.'
Dr Katalin Gaal, Editor

Herlinde Cayzer is a Brisbane-based writer with a PhD in German Language and Literature. Her articles and reviews have appeared in anthologies and online publications. She is a snippeter who blogs her short stories, musings, and reviews about the arts at:

herlindesnippets.blogspot.com

sepia

If only he hadn't. If only she had.

Herlinde Cayzer

First Published – 2022

This edition published 2022 by Herlinde Cayzer
Brisbane, Qld Australia
herlindesnippets.blogspot.com

Copyright © Herlinde Cayzer 2022

The National Library of Australia Cataloguing-in-Publication

Creator: Cayzer, Herlinde, author.

Title: *sepia. If only he hadn't. If only she had.* / Herlinde Cayzer.

ISBN: 978-0-6452737-0-0 (paperback)

Subjects: Historical fiction.
                      General fiction
                      Australian fiction.
                      German fiction.
                      World War II

I acknowledge the Traditional Owners and their custodianship of country
throughout Australia. I pay my respects to their Ancestors and their descendants,
who continue cultural and spiritual connections to Country. I recognise their
valuable contributions to Australian and global society.

Typeset in Times New Roman 12pt.
Cover artwork by Donna Munro Graphic Design.
Author photograph by Hannah Photography.
Printed and bound in Australia by Ingram Spark.

Contents

Map of Germany

You can't always swim against the current,
but you always have to have enough character
not to get carried away.
- Curt Goetz

Prologue

'Don't you know? We've lost. The war is over. Man.'

Grimacing in pain, Heinz clutched his chest and slumped onto the rubble. Propped up on his left elbow, he stared in disbelief into Werner's face. Slowly but incessantly, the blood trickled out of the corner of Heinz's parted lips, as he exhaled, 'You fool.'

Heinz's last words were to haunt Werner for the rest of his life. If only he hadn't blindly followed the battalion leader's instructions on that fateful day on the third of May 1945, so close to the war's end.

If only—how many times are these two words uttered? Probably seldom with the immense regret Werner felt. He could not help his father's death, nor his mother's, nor Anna's. But he could have prevented his best friend's.

1. Sigrid, Werner, Heinz

Sigrid 2013

Sigrid wrestled out of her *heavenly* hammock and steadied herself. Picking up her book and cup of tea, she cautiously stepped along the pavers surrounding the lap pool and proceeded along the path towards the living room of her cottage. As usual, when entering, she glanced wistfully at the photo in the carved wooden frame on top of the bookshelf. *Still looking after me, even when you're not with me.* Over the years, the urge to demystify the tragic event from her childhood in Germany had not lost its intensity. But now, Isabella was due to arrive, and Sigrid was determined to enjoy the next few days with her granddaughter.

Immersed in the murmur of the crowds at Brisbane airport, Sigrid scrutinised the flight arrival display board.

'Hi, Oma.'

Turning to her right, Sigrid was taken back by the spectacular vision of a vibrant pink and purple striped shirt a split second before registering Isabella's broadly smiling face.

'Oh, darling, how nice to see you again.'

They hugged warmly, kissing cheeks, laughing.

'How you have grown since I last saw you. Look at us. You are taller than me now.'

Stepping back, Sigrid gushed further, 'Oh, let me look at you again. You are getting more and more beautiful. You look great darling. I'm so happy to see you. Did you have a good flight from Gladstone? Let's go and collect your luggage from the carousel.'

Unable to get a word in and glancing around surreptitiously to check if anyone was watching, Isabella pressed her lips together and mumbled, 'Yeah, well…'

They went down the airport escalator, arm in arm to collect Isabella's psychedelically coloured suitcase. One could be forgiven for thinking this was the 1960s and not the twenty-first century. That is Isabella. A gorgeous young creature.

During the drive home, they chatted excitedly, clearly enjoying each other's company. While Sigrid's relationship with her daughter Katrina was more formal, she was at ease with Isabella. Spoiling her granddaughter ensured a certain endearment but isn't that one of the privileges that come with being Oma? Moreover, her affection came naturally—almost like old age. But while the former was a delight, Sigrid felt the latter to be a persistently challenging nuisance.

Sigrid was aware of her physical appeal, particularly while travelling through Europe. There, the political correctness that seemed to have swept Australia was refreshingly vague. To this day, she continued to relish a young Frenchman's, *Mais oui, Madame, you arr verrie attrakktiff.* Being slim, *attractive*, and naturally flirtatious, she enjoyed the banter with male members of society. Sigrid's short white hair framed an oval face from which deep blue eyes twinkled. The slight gap between her front teeth projected a cheeky smile and the few neck wrinkles did not detract.

Approaching the cottage, the gushing switched to Isabella, 'Oh, Oma, how lovely your place looks. How are the chooks?'

'You'll see them in a minute. Let me just park the car.'

They drove towards the garage. Schatzi, the smooth-haired Dachshund, yelped welcomingly between circling, running and jumping along the driveway. Schatzi too was happy to see Isabella, even though her ball games were more energetic than the little canine was used to. Gertie, Bertie and Floss were busy picking up worms, insects, grubs and other tidbits in the ground and did not take too much notice of the young visitor.

Over dinner, Isabella told Sigrid about her school trip to Germany, scheduled for next year but already eagerly discussed in class.

'We'll be leaving in November and returning in January. Just imagine a white Christmas. I have never seen snow before. It's going to be so exciting. And our teacher said the same as you about the *Christkindlmarkt* in Nürnberg. I can hardly wait, Oma. It's so good you're helping me with my German homework. All the stories and history. It does help, you know. And when I'm in Year Ten—I'm actually going. Yay.'

'Yes, it is exciting. And it will be wonderful for you to be immersed in the language and culture. That is, not only of your ancestors, but also the language you are studying at school.' Lowering her tone as if to confide, Sigrid continued, 'You know, we are so remote here in Australia. In Europe you only travel a short distance and you are in another country with a different language and customs. Here you travel long distances and it's all the same. I know,' she inhaled for a breather, 'some may argue that there is a difference between a North Queenslander and an urban Victorian, but—ah, that's another matter. Anyway, it'll be good for you and I'm so pleased.'

With the slightest touch of sadness, Sigrid softly added, 'I've always dreamed of going with you one day. Well, maybe another time.'

While Sigrid cleared the dishes, Isabella stroked the small carved squirrel on top of the bookshelf. 'So cute, Oma calls you *Knusperchen*,' she mumbled while scanning the old photograph to its left, which always captured her attention on each visit. She carefully picked up the wooden frame and studied the sepia outline of the two youngsters.

'Oma, I know this is you and your brother Heinz. How old were you here?'

'I'd just turned seven and Heinz was thirteen. Same age as you are now. He would have been your mum's uncle.' After a moment, pointing her index finger mid-air, she added, 'That was the last time I saw him. It was my birthday.'

Coming closer, she dried her hands, pointed to the squirrel, and continued, 'As you know, Heinz sculpted *Knusperchen* for me. The next day he rowed me over the lake to the magical castle of Schwerin.'

Wiping her right eye with the back of her hand, she quivered slightly, 'Then, not even a year later, he was killed. It was tragic. Sad.' She took a deep breath. 'And the war was over. Can you believe it? So sad and ironic.'

'I am sorry.'

Isabella hesitated, contemplating the puzzle surrounding this photo and her granduncle ever since she was old enough to understand. She pressed on softly, 'What actually happened?'

'I really don't know. It was all such a mystery. And Mother, your great grandmother Emilie, was utterly grieved. I guess at the time, I was too young to understand.' With resolve she added, 'You see, my father died next. But before that, Heinz had been sent to various Hitler Youth camps. At that time, they did that with all the boys over the age of ten. So, I never saw that much of him anyway.' She wiped both eyes.

'The times were wicked, horrible, people never coming back. Bombs dropping. Everyone running into air-raid shelters.' Sigrid blew her nose, looked into her granddaughter's eyes, and resumed with composure, 'I am so glad you don't have to grow up in such horridness.'

With a sigh, Sigrid ran her right hand along the photo frame. More collected, she continued, 'As I said, I was so young, but when I saw him, Heinz always looked after me and he told me that he would.' She hesitated, 'But that was not to be.'

Closely studying the boy in the photograph, Isabella concluded, 'What a shame you never found out what happened. You both look happy, and he looks so kind.'

'Oh, yes, that he was.' Sigrid paused, with a lump in her throat and tears welling again as she emphasised, 'He was.' After all those years, the pain still surfaced easily whenever she thought about her brother. The inexplicable circumstances surrounding his early death always triggered the same ache. Turning around, she busied herself at the kitchen sink.

Changing from the lugubrious tone, she called over her shoulder, 'If you like, tomorrow we could go to the art gallery in the city.'

'Oh, yes. Yes, I'd like that. That would be good. In fact, we're studying artists of the nineteenth-century at school.'

'Hmm, I thought you'd be interested. You were always pretty good at art, even when you were little. I've still got one of the first drawings you made for me.'

'I would also like to go to the museum to see an exhibition of the two-thousand-year-old treasures from Afghanistan. I read about it in the *Qantas* magazine on the plane.'

'I've seen it. It's fabulous. You'll love it. When would you like to see that?'

'Maybe the day after tomorrow?'

'Ah, that is the day I usually see my friend David.' As soon as she said it, Sigrid regretted she blurted it out. How could she forget to cancel? She quickly continued, 'Oh, but I'll give him a ring and call it off.'

'No, please don't do that because of me. And you've already seen the exhibition anyway.'

'No problem at all. I'd much rather spend time with you, my sweet.'

'But Oma, I've got my sketchbook and I would really like to copy some of the designs. I always spend time by myself doing that. So, please go and see your friend. You can drop me off and pick me up later. I'm not a little girl, you know.'

'Alright, if you're happy with that, then that's what we'll do.'

Without further planning, they settled down on the couch and started leafing through various art books. Sigrid played Carmen Maria Vega's CD *On S'en Font,* starting with the rhythm-banging track *Singe Savant* with which she wanted to impress her young visitor.

'Oh, Oma, you're so, so cool.'

Sigrid smiled triumphantly.

Werner 2013

Absorbing Yo-Yo Ma playing the Prélude from Bach's Suite No. 1 in G Major, Werner did not immediately notice Eva enter his study bringing a cup of tea and a shortbread biscuit, both on a small oval-shaped saucer.

'Thank you, dear, that will do just nicely.'

'Werner, you are brooding too much. I'm worried about you. Perhaps we should've stayed in Wodonga. You had loyal patients, who became your friends.'

He'd heard that a few times and did not feel like starting a conversation about it again but to pacify his dear wife of many years, he answered curtly, 'Yes, but you know my arthritis is not as crippling as it used to be. Besides, you too enjoy the climate here in Queensland. You have a nice home. You've got your book club friends. You are involved with the fundraising organisation that raises money for melanoma research.' He paused, *'Apricity*. We go to concerts and movies. You've got me, and, after all—you are Frau Doctor Mueller—anglicised with the letters 'ue' and not the original German 'ü' *Umlaut*. What more could you wish for?'

Werner could not control using the Teutonic formality of not only addressing her as 'Mrs' but elevating her onto a higher social platform with his doctor title.

Eva, having heard this before, knew not to get into any further pointless discussion.

'Yes, dear.'

She left the room and him to it.

Werner looked through the window over his pine tree planted against Eva's many protests when they first moved to The Gap. He dunked the biscuit into his tea and allowed his mind to wander back to the years of his childhood in Germany. His earliest memory was of the garden at his grandmother's.

Oma's apple tree

The apple tree was in the centre of her garden, in fact, it was the centre of all visits to his oma. As he grew older, his mother would always hide coloured eggs in one of its boughs at Easter. That was the time just before the little pink-white blossoms appeared everywhere. He remembered a few years later climbing the big branch so that he could jump onto the grass below. He pretended to be Uli, the character in Erich Kästner's *The Flying Classroom* who, to demonstrate his courage in the gymnasium jumped with an umbrella from a great height. Uli broke his leg but basked in the recognition of being celebrated as a hero by his school friends. Werner did not break his leg and instead of heroic recognition, he got a smack from his father together with a stern reprimand to never do such a stupid thing again.

During summer, this apple tree had a seat attached to two ropes on which his sister Anna often swung as hard and high as she could.

Oma would call out, 'Gentle, Anna, gentle, slow down. You'll slip and hurt yourself. Remember what happened to your brother.'

But Anna was wild and fearless. With her white-blond curls she flew through the air, laughing and shouting, 'Higher. Faster. It's nice.' Werner loved his little sister; she was everything he was not: lively, cheeky, confronting and very headstrong. The only trait they shared was a sense of inquisitiveness, though his was of a more earnest nature. If Anna did not want to tidy up her room, she did not and that was the end of it. Even Father could not cajole her, and she was the apple of his eye, whether she was swinging in the tree or not. With her big brown eyes, her pout and her tantrums, she got away with everything. It was not really fair, but that was Anna. Dear little Anna, who died far too young.

Werner's childhood progressed with some normality until his sixth birthday. He remembered painstakingly copying *Montag, 4.4.1938* onto his slate on his first day at school. At home, Mother was looking after him and Anna while Father was still living there. During the early years, after Hitler's *Kabinett* had introduced compulsory military service, life for the Müller family seemed to continue as before. But Werner remembered his uncle Otto whisper to Father, 'I knew dark times would descend upon us when Hitler assumed control and dissolved the coalition government. And then the arsonists burnt the Reichstag building in 1933.'

'What do you mean, Otto?' his agitated father responded. 'We do have law and order now. We do have bread on the table. Remember the times when we didn't? When things go well for you, you easily forget. Don't you?'

Father had always worked in the police force, which to this day Werner still associates with the smell of shiny black leather boots. Back then, Werner would sit at his father's feet and study the crown motif imprinted on the ribbed black heel. He often asked to shine his father's service boots.

But one year later, Father's little group of law protectors merged into a larger police regiment. Soon after the *Wehrmacht's* Blitzkrieg on Poland in 1939, Father was sent to join the Western offensive against France. He occasionally visited when leave was granted, but chaos had already descended. The normality of civilian life was diminished by militarism. One day, Father was sent to Norway. Mother was very upset but not as upset as when he was sent to the Russian Front. By then, a general sense of fanaticism vacillated with that of despair. For Werner, life at school had lost its orderliness.

The ringing of the phone disturbed Werner's ruminations. By the time he turned his swivel armchair, the calling stopped. Eva must have answered. Werner pondered that his wife, though born in Australia, also had scars from the war.

Eva Prenzler originally came from Hahndorf in South Australia. She knew a few German words when she first met Werner, but was too shy to speak them. Her father, Gustav had been a pastor. During the Second World War, the Australian Government interned the family because of their German heritage. The fact that Gustav was born in Adelaide did not give the Prenzlers any privileges. This internment, the act of racial dislike and isolation, left Eva feeling ostracised, turned off religion, and scarred for life. To this day, she does not discuss her ancestry and still has problems spelling out her birth name. Yet her anglicised married name of 'Mueller' is not less German, especially with a preceding Doctor title. But, to Eva, this was better than Prenzler. If she referred to her background at all, it was by mentioning her aunt Ruth in England as though Eva came from there.

The mournful irony here is that during the English *Operation Gomorrah* Werner's mother and sister were killed. That was war in all its atrocity, involving innocent civilians sheltering from the falling bombs. It was terrible then and it is terrible now in Iraq, Afghanistan, Egypt, Sri Lanka, and so many other places. Has humankind learned anything? Not from the mistakes of their fathers and forebearers. No, each generation knows it all and knows it better. They know how to develop weapons that become deadlier and more precise, to such an extent that they can shoot targets in Afghanistan from their headquarters in another country.

Werner was glad that he did not have children. Eva would have liked to, but Werner's turbulent youth culminating with his final deed of misguided lunacy at the end of the war in Germany had removed any desire to be the head of a family.

He proceeded to take another sip from the now cold tea, thought for a split second, put the cup aside, then went to his wall cabinet to pick up a bottle of *Jägermeister*. Pouring a generous shot into a tumbler, Werner allowed his nostrils to inhale the herbal scent before savouring the dark-brown liqueur.

Sliding into a comfortable position, he again thought about the majestic pine tree on the front lawn. He and Eva did have a few arguments on that subject. The neighbours were not happy either as it would obstruct their view, but he did not care. It was his plot, his lot, and he liked the pine tree, stubbornly magnificent and solitary. Out of place, really, where it stood. So, what? It was his tree and reminded him of Germany. A relaxed feeling spread throughout his limbs, and again his mind returned to his childhood.

The Battle of Stalingrad in 1943 had terrible consequences for all involved. And for the Müller household, it was particularly and personally tragic when the government letter arrived to inform them that Werner's father had died during that battle in January. The mandatory 'He died as a hero for his *Führer* and Fatherland' was little consolation for his grieving family.

One year before this devastating news, Werner's life had already taken a tumultuous turn. When he was ten, Werner, like every other ten-year-old boy, was drafted into the first category of the Hitler Youth organisation (*HJ*) as a cub (*Pf*) of the Young People of Germany organisation (*DJV*). It was the omnipresent *HJ's* task to integrate the youth of Germany into a useful link of Hitler's national socialistic (*NS*) machinery, which abided by the dictate, 'He, who has youth following, gains the future.' Accordingly, the young boys were drilled with iron determination to follow without hesitation this *NS* doctrine. It promulgated the value of instructing children in teamwork and camaraderie to make their dogma palatable to those parents who may not welcome the *NS* regime with enthusiastic approval.

Apart from this ideological change in life, Werner's disrupted school years took an even greater turn when he was sent to Linz in Austria as part of the government regulated dispatch of children to the country (*KLV*). To safeguard the future of Germany's young generation, children were sent to areas deemed to be 'safe' during the war. More than two million children from air-raid targeted cities were sent all over the Third Reich. Still only ten years of age, Werner ended up with the ominously named Austrian teacher couple, Herr and Frau Schreck (Fright).

Werner was terribly homesick; being unable to understand the local Austrian dialect in school did not help. Even though he was bright and quick to learn, he was an outsider, different, foreign. Getting a hiding in the school ground from the other boys in his class was the least of his agonies. He did not ask to be sent there, nor for Austria to be annexed to the German Reich. He did not want to be in Linz.

Years later, he remained tormented by the painful nights at the Schrecks. When locked in the narrow spare room, he could not get to the toilet and, in agonising desperation, urinated into the corner pot which held Frau Schreck's treasured rubber plant. No, he had no memories of an Austria that vocalised *The Sound of Music*. What he retained was devoid of any alpine exuberance.

Werner saw Mother and Anna for the last time in Hamburg before he was transported in the middle of June 1943 under the jurisdiction of the Hitler Youth to the second 'safe' location, a camp in Malchin, in the state of Mecklenburg. As it was still summer school holidays, he was supposed to stay in Hamburg until the end of the vacation, after which he was scheduled to go to Malchin. Due to a rare administrative error, the national socialist welfare for the people (*NSVW*) had organised his transport to take place before the end of his holiday. An error that was to save his life.

During the last days of these vacations, Mother had become quiet. She was grieving Father and worrying about her two children. Against all odds, she managed to keep Anna with her, the exception being when the *NSVW* forced her to send Anna to a foster family on a farm in Prussia. Mother tried to escape to Oma's garden as often as possible, but her duty to work in the ammunition factory became increasingly pressing and consuming. When not in the country with a care family, Anna irregularly attended school in Hamburg.

Werner treasured the memory of their last time together. He would often lie in bed and recall how Mother managed to make three pancakes filled with sliced apples. She boiled a few drops of red wine and water with cinnamon and sugar. She lit four candles, an extra one for Father. The loss of Father weighed heavily with all of them. Yet they managed to share a few memorable moments of love, belonging and togetherness.

Eventually, the air raid alarm with its wailing siren blared, as it did most nights. Mother grabbed her two children and the little suitcase with personal documents. Like the other tenants of the building, the three raced into the cellar for shelter, where they huddled together on plank beds as the bombs fell.

The next morning the damage and debris were massive. Miraculously their block was yet again unscathed.

In late afternoon Mother embraced Werner at the railway station and did not want to let him go. Perhaps she had an inkling that it was to be for the last time. Anna too had lost her earlier vibrancy; her cheeks were no longer rosy. She disliked the sleep-deprived nights, the sirens, running for shelter, the queues, and her forced stays in the backwoods. There was little left of her earlier stubbornness. She had grown up far too quickly. With tears in her eyes, her last words to Werner were, 'Till next time, big brother.'

Days later, in Malchin, the Hitler Youth leader called Werner aside to give him the news that his mother and Anna had been killed. *Operation Gomorrah* had created one of the largest firestorms ever raised by the RAF and USAAF in July 1943. It destroyed most of Hamburg. During the bombing, Werner's mother and Anna took refuge in an air-raid shelter under Karstadt, the large department store. They and so many other innocent people lost their lives through heat and carbon monoxide poisoning. Within one year, eleven-year-old Werner lost his entire family. His oma had already died from a heart attack the year before.

For a few brief months in his life, despite losing his family, Werner experienced a feeling of friendship and trust with his new friend Heinz. Heinz was to die because of Werner's misled judgment, an incident that was to haunt him forever. In 1945 Werner was thirteen, the war had ended, and he lost the best friend ever.

Germany was in chaos. Displaced people and refugees were everywhere: destruction, rubble and dirt, burnt-out ruins, distrust, fear, hunger, pain, loss and anguish. How he had managed to find his way through all this debris to Uncle Otto in Hamburg Lokstedt still amazed Werner.

Hoping to obliterate the extremely painful memory of his involvement in Heinz's death, Werner left Hamburg in his early twenties to follow the Australian Government's call for European tradesmen to work on the Snowy Mountain Scheme in the 1950s. The economy at that time was still grim in Germany. Australia was far enough to create at least a symbolic distance from his involvement in that dreadful event at the end of the war.

Eva entered his room again. Werner noted that she was dressed to go out.

'I'll be off now, dear.'

'Where are you going?'

'I've got an *Apricity* meeting in Milton.'

'Have fun.'

'Thanks, dear.' Eva left the room and closed the door, not so gently.

Ħeinz - Germany 1939–1944

When the war broke out, Heinz was eight years old. He lived with his parents, Emilie and Wilhelm Hermes, and his two-year-old sister, Sigrid, in a spacious three-roomed apartment on the third floor in Berlin, Schmargendorf. In summer, the western facade was a wall of green, overgrown with ivy, as was so often the case with apartment blocks in Berlin. Sometimes a sparrow would land on the windowsill and peck around the leafy foliage. But no matter how carefully Heinz planned his approach, he could never catch one, not even with the butterfly net that his opa had given him a few years earlier. Being athletically talented, Heinz liked outdoor physical activity. When he was not playing marbles in the inner courtyard or climbing up the chestnut trees on the outer footpath, Heinz watched the street happenings below from his window.

Although Schrammstrasse was not on a major road, its activities provided sufficient entertainment for the fertile mind of its young spectator, at least until Mother called Heinz to do a chore, usually to mind Sigrid, or get forgotten food ingredients at the corner store. One of the highlights in the street was when old Herr Habermann returned with his horse. He lived on the ground floor adjacent to the thoroughfare leading to the apartment building at the back. This arrangement enabled the sprightly gentleman to have a set-up resembling a stall for his horse. Herr Habermann was one of the few people who still conducted a horse and carriage enterprise. And here, Jakob, his horse, lived, slept, ate hay and drank water when not being out on one of his master's trotting engagements. Each evening, Herr Habermann brushed Jakob's coat with strong, loving, yet amazingly tender strokes.

Whenever Heinz's mother gave him a lump of sugar, Herr Habermann allowed the young boy to feed it to Jakob. To enable him in this task, Heinz climbed onto a wooden stool, stretched out his small hand as flat as he could and tried to stand as still as possible so that he could be very close to the animal. On tiptoes, Heinz put his nose onto the horse's neck to breathe in the horsey smell, which gave him a feeling of warmth and comfort. One day he would have a horse of his own, just like Jakob; he felt sure of it. Often it is best to indulge in one's dreams in utter devotion, for they provide hope while the knowledge of what some wretched future holds is best kept unknown.

Heinz made reasonable progress in his third year at the local primary school. At this stage, school life was still conducted with some sense of orderliness and routine. Heinz liked his class teacher Herr Buhl, but being shy, kept his distance. He was not like some of the pushy boys. Heinz's favourite subject was Physical Education. He enjoyed vaulting in the gymnasium. He loved the freedom to run around with a purpose, be it propelling himself into the air, catching a ball or kicking a football. Heinz also liked to draw and enjoyed copying into his sketchbook outlines of countries from the big world map at the back of the classroom. His grades in oral and written German reached an average level. The other boys generally liked him; in his grey shorts, with customary long socks and a dark shirt, he was one of the group and did not really distinguish himself through any outer variance. His sandy hair was parted on his right, leaving a long strand of hair covering half his brow. With a ready smile, a sassy glint in his eyes and a slightly upturned nose, he was streetwise, and pleasant to be around.

Wilhelm Hermes recognised his son's aptitude towards reproducing what he saw in sketches, which prompted him to give Heinz an Agfa Synchro Box Camera and a developing kit for his tenth birthday. Herr Hermes told four-year-old Sigrid to give her brother the small parcel that held a roll of film. Incredibly happy with his new camera, Heinz snapped Jakob, trees, birds, apartment blocks, Sigrid, marbles in the distance and close-up. His hobby took much of his energy, especially after he learned how to develop the shots in the darkened bathroom. With great care, he would open the Agfa Box and prudently remove the film, which he then cautiously slid over a reel, trimming off the excess. After swaying the film from side to side through the developer mix, he rinsed it with water and pinned it tenderly onto a drying line. When the negative was ready to develop, Heinz mixed the developer and watched the white paper anxiously for smudges to appear to then become an image. The hours he spent with this pastime helped forge his thoughtfulness and patience.

However, the Hermes's domestic routine was increasingly eroded by external factors. When Germany attacked Poland, most of the population were still too traumatised from the horrors of the First World War to show real enthusiasm for this raid. In awareness of people's reluctance to participate in this new war, the National Socialist (*NS*) regime phased in compulsory rationing, first food then clothing. Like an impenetrable black curtain pulled over the sky, life for the non-political citizens became more regimented and restricted. Those politically involved welcomed these changes with enthusiastic fervour. Schools received orders to take part in the war effort and send whole classes into the country to help with the harvest, mass collections of iron and distribute *NS*-propaganda material. More and more pro-regime demonstrations were first expected and then demanded to show a willingness to make sacrifices in the spirit of solidarity and for the good of the national community. It became a regular expectation to donate to the war effort.

After his tenth birthday, Heinz was drafted into his age-appropriate section of the Hitler Youth (*DJV*). Yet even in the ballooning chaos of the time, he experienced moments of boyish bliss. One afternoon, Heinz followed two older boys from his apartment block to the cinema. Copying their lead, Heinz managed to sneak into the cinema where they watched *Quax der Bruchpilot*, the heroic derring-do pilot who was inclined to have accidents. What excitement. Inspired by Quax's adventures, Heinz too yearned to become a pilot. He could barely contain his emotions. Running home, rushing into his building block, he simply had to shout into the courtyard, 'Mutter, Mutter, guess what? I went to the movies. I saw Quax, the pilot, and I didn't even pay for it.'

Taking two steps at a time, he entered the apartment breathlessly.

'Heinz. Don't shout all over the *Hinterhof* (inner courtyard) that you didn't pay for the movies,' Mother said.

'I don't want the whole neighbourhood to hear that.' She pointed her index finger at him. 'How did you do it anyway? I thought you were in the park playing with Rudi.'

She tried not to show her bemusement too openly and did not begrudge her son a few hours of harmless entertainment. Mother could not afford to give him the money for a ticket; she had to scrape and budget to make ends meet. Indeed, weeks later, the Hermes family experienced the first personal changes that would disrupt their lives forever. A draft card arrived, calling Heinz's father to fight for the *Führer* and the Fatherland on the Eastern Front. Somehow Mother hoped that Father would be spared. In the suppressing atmosphere of Nazi euphoria, she did not dare to voice a hope that was considered to be treasonous. The ultimate stages of political madness descended and encroached on their existence like an unstoppable tsunami. In response to Germany's invasion of Poland, the attack on German cities increased. After the first British air raids, more and more bombs fell on Berlin, burying an increasing number of civilians under the rubble.

As part of the same government-regulated dispatch of children to the country *(KLV)* that had sent Werner to Linz in Austria, Heinz was sent with all of Herr Buhl's class to Berchtesgaden in Bavaria. On his day of departure, Berlin's central railway station was awash with school students boarding the train. The pain of saying goodbye to Mother and his sister Sigrid gave way to the general excitement of seeing snow-covered alpine regions for the first time. In between the unfamiliar surroundings and feeling homesick, Heinz gazed in awe at the mountainous spectacle.

The panorama of gleaming white snow against the stark blue sky gave Heinz new respect for nature. The air was so pure and fresh, and the snow glistened like silver, not tinged with grey and black. Whenever he could get away from classroom teaching and mountain survival skills training, Heinz enjoyed hiking into the high-altitude, watching eagles fly and chamois climb. Sometimes he tried to follow the Capricorns with their incredibly curved horns, but they remained elusive, for either the creatures were too fast, or somebody would call out, 'Hey, Heinz, where ya off to? Come back. Herr Buhl wants you. NOW.'

And what did Herr Buhl want Heinz for? Nothing really. The boys just didn't want Heinz to experience something they were not a part of. What did all this Hitler Youth teaching about camaraderie prove? Don't be an individualist. Conform, be part of the herd and its collective blindly following mentality. How well the children responded beyond the reach and influence of their parents—Heinz being somewhat of an exception.

Herr Buhl's class remained in Berchtesgaden for over twelve months, and the majority felt privileged to be in proximity to the *Führer's* headquarters. Indeed, one day on the twentieth of April, Heinz's Year Five class and many other classes had a day off school to march into the village in anticipation of greeting the *Führer* and wishing him a happy birthday. Having been inculcated with his precept of being 'tough like leather, and hard like Krupp steel,' they waited the whole day, but Herr Hitler must have had a more pressing engagement as he never came and probably stipulated young minds should be malleable, and forget, if not forgive.

By the time Heinz returned in 1943, Berlin was transformed. The railway system had been extensively damaged. More than a quarter of the suburbs were rendered unlivable. The air was thick with dust and smog. Surprisingly Schrammstrasse was still recognisable. While some apartment blocks had collapsed into a pile of debris, Heinz's corner still stood undamaged. Mother was relieved to have her son back, and Sigrid too, was happy to cuddle into her big brother. She seemed to be more grown-up with her two light-brown plaits. 'I really missed you. What was it like in the mountains? Were they covered in snow? How high are they? Did you climb any? There has been so much bombing going on here. Every night into the shelter, I'm tired of it.'

'I wish you could've come with me. It was good, but you know, there were no littlies like you.'

'I'm not little. I'm already six, you know.' Slightly miffed, she added, 'You did miss my birthday.'

'Enough, you two. Let's sort things out before it gets dark,' interjected Mother and placed the evening meal on the table.

'Have you heard from Father?'

'Yes, my boy. He's still on the Eastern Front. He came home for about two weeks and then had to go back again,' answered Mother with an unmistakable tremble in her voice. They ate their cabbage and potatoes in silence. Despite being home, Heinz missed the juicy Bavarian cheese *Spätzle* but stopped himself just in time from saying it. He did not want to upset Mother in an already slightly tense atmosphere.

'We can't stay in Berlin. The bombing is getting worse, and we are just exhausted running into the shelter just about every night,' Mother said.

'Where're we going?' asked Sigrid.

'I'm working on something,' Mother replied wearily. 'When the directive arrives for Heinz to go to one of the school camps, we two,' pointing to Sigrid and then herself, 'will try to move somewhere close by so that we're not too far apart from each other. We're all worn out. Tired. All those sirens. Picking up the ready packed cases at the front door. Checking our Aryan passports, the documents, the little valuables.' Inhaling, she emphasised, 'And I am just sick, so very sick of running into those stuffy sardine-packed cellars.'

Soon after, a notification arrived to advise Heinz of his place in a school camp in Malchin. As Mother's sister Rosemarie lived in nearby Schwerin, it did not take long for Mother's enthusiastic, 'I'll ask your aunt if she has room for Sigrid and me. I'm sure she does. At least we'll be close to each other. We just have to organise the transport. It might be difficult, but we'll find a way.'

Heinz heaved a sigh, 'I'm sure you will, Mother.'

Sigrid contemplated if she would see snow-capped mountains there.

2. Australia 2013

Sigrid and Isabella

After breakfast, grandmother and granddaughter drove to the State Art Gallery in the city. When they entered the room displaying paintings from previous centuries, Sigrid proudly observed Isabella's obvious joy and absorption of Angelika Kauffmann's *The Deserted Costanza*.

'Oma, you can really see the fear and confusion on her face. Even the doom is there.'

'Yes, you can,' Sigrid answered happily. *All my earbashing about this artist has had an effect.* Sigrid had given Isabella a Kauffmann book for her tenth birthday. *Perhaps, at that age prematurely? But no, I don't think so now.*

Isabella faced Sigrid, 'I loved your story of how Angelika was one of the few female painters who made her living through her art in the eighteenth century.'

'That's right, darling. She had gained recognition and her name is preserved in European art history. She was one of the women I featured in my teaching about the emancipatory struggle of women from earlier centuries. Most of them were writers, but she was one of the few painters.'

They moved from paintings and sculptures to the glassed display units, viewing, reading, absorbing and contemplating their surroundings.

Lunch at the gallery

'Let's have some lunch over there.' Sigrid pointed ahead, 'At the gallery café. My feet are aching.'

Isabella followed. They sat around one of the gallery café's tables. Three pools with water features and fountains created a tranquil atmosphere. Dappled light shone through the canopy of the Tipuana trees. The reflection of its branches danced gently on the water's surface. A scrumptious light salad complemented the arty excursion.

'Oma, I really like the sculptures down there. They look so randomly placed, but they are aesthetically positioned.' With a smirk she added, 'You like my new vocab? Aesthetic?'

'Wow, yes, I am impressed. Very sophisticated.'

'I'm just going to have a closer look at that bronze lady over there.'

Isabella bounced down the grassed contour line.

For no apparent reason, the blue sky against this predominantly leafy setting reminded Sigrid of her visit to Heiligendamm on the Baltic Sea two years earlier.

It was the beginning of June, a lovely time of year in Europe. I remember taking the train from Hamburg to Bad Doberan, where I boarded Molli, the narrow-gauge steam-powered train for the six-kilometre railway ride to Heiligendamm. How it always amused me to see men, both young and old, excitedly wave their cameras and other gadgets to inspect Molli at close range. Children and mothers animatedly fussed around the platform as well and, if I am honest with myself—I did too. There is something magical about old steam trains, huffing and puffing through the differently coloured shades of forest green. Molli stopped at that majestic complex of the Grand Hotel Heiligendamm, the oldest sea bath and resort in Germany. Throughout the centuries, the upper classes had enjoyed times of leisure and pleasure there. What a life! From the little station platform, I could see the rear of the hotel complex that, true to its name, was grand.

Heiligendamm on the Baltic Sea

A big low-set main building, probably the original 'Kurhaus' (assembly room at a health resort), was set between two three-storey buildings. I remember so well how all the buildings were snow white and contrasted the red-tiled roof of the centre building. The whole complex was surrounded by manicured lawns, a brilliant blue sky and a blue-green sea. That never-ending Baltic Sea. How I loved it. None of the hotels I ever stayed in were as magnificent in their setting, architecture or exclusiveness as the Grand Hotel. From the moment I entered the reception, I felt pampered. The sitting room and bedroom of my suite were extremely spacious, with glorious views over the enticing water.

The bathroom—a dream in gold and marble. The service—impeccable. The menus of the various restaurants—equally impressive. Leaving my shoes to be polished in a basket outside my door at night—thrilling. Being built right on the sea—oh so therapeutic. This was a life that I could have easily become accustomed to. No wonder Heiligendamm was referred to as the White Town by the Sea. To me, it was like the Grand Dame. A bit like me, really. Ha-ha, as if! She breathed deeply. *Of course, that's why the thirty-third G8 summit took place there in 2007.*

Taking another sip of coffee, Sigrid indulged in further pondering.

I still like to visit as often as I can, even though I am no longer actively involved in teaching my native language and the cultural aspects of Germany to student in Brisbane. And I am so pleased Isabella shows an interest. I'm sure she'll take it to a higher level on her immersion into the German culture during her school visit. In fact, in a couple of years, I hope that one day I can show Isabella the finer aspects of her heritage, like the bathing culture of Heiligendamm, for example. I can just see us lounging in a 'Strandkorb', the traditional roofed-wicker beach chair, soaking up the air, the waves, the wind, the sounds of the birds, the whole atmosphere, and of course, partake in a bit of bubbly.

Perhaps Sigrid's vision about being involved in Isabella's future would materialise. However, many a grandmother had similar aspirations shattered, forgetting that young people have a mind of their own and their planning scheme does not necessarily include family members. This applied in particular to grandmothers, no matter how 'so, so cool' they might be.

Sigrid was roused out of her daydreams.

'If you'd like to go now, Oma, that's fine with me.'

'Alright, I'll pay the bill and we'll go home.'

They left the art gallery's café for the trip back.

The next morning, after dropping Isabella at the museum, Sigrid enjoyed the drive along St Lucia's winding and narrow tree-lined roads to David's house. Some of the trees were still bare, but the pale purple of the first jacarandas already dotted the blue sky of spring. The hedges of manicured evergreen murrayas and lilly pillies lined the streets. Passing the school just before the last roundabout, she wondered in what frame of mind she would find her dear old friend.

David

Sigrid reflected on meeting David for the first time at a dinner that Dimitry, her Russian friend, *with the piercing blue eyes and long jet-black hair,* gave at his place eight months earlier. David's fine features had captivated Sigrid. His alert eyes were set in a handsomely oval face. He was in his mid-seventies, with a well-proportioned slimness and a sharp and insightfully entertaining intellect. During the main course, the focus of the conversation turned to her and Rainer Maria Rilke.

She recalled her reaction, 'Oh, yes, he is an exquisite German poet. Yes, I know his "The Notebooks of Malte Laurids Brigge." Sure, I can read a paragraph in the original language.'

All the lights of the crystal chandelier burst into illumination—*so* that, *and not my good looks—was the reason for the invite. Thanks, Dimitry.*

The proposed passage looked like half a page in length. *Well, yes, why not? I pull that kind of trick at any banquet.* Sigrid's throat was suddenly devoid of moisture. She felt the pressure. *Ok, here we go.*

Sigrid understood she had read to an audience of literati and hesitantly awaited their approval of her skill to emphasise certain phraseology, intonation or expression. After all, she had never read Rilke. But Sigrid passed the test, as David invited her the following week to his place to read and debate Heinrich Heine's epic satirical poem *Germany: A Winter's Tale.*

Sigrid mused with fondness about her friend. The scholar, who had cultivated his eccentricity from an early age. David was born in Calcutta but was sent to boarding school in England. After finishing his degree, he travelled extensively and taught in England, where he married. His love for the humanities led him to Australia, where the Queensland University employed him as a Professor of English Literature. David's wife had died from cancer some years later, but every day he still placed a freshly picked stalk of red geranium into a small vessel in front of her photograph. After an operation to remove a tumorous growth in his stomach, David's once-solid frame had shrunk. He now ate sparingly, avoided fatty foods, but still enjoyed alcoholic beverages.

Since his retirement, David's thirst for intellectual stimuli did not diminish, maintaining his immersion in literature. He attracted good numbers for his poetry classes at the University of the Third Age, remarking, 'I love poetry. It is precise, no word is wasted.' While avoiding small talk, David loved to indulge in his daily ritual at five o'clock of having a smooth Scotch with olives, cheese and nuts. That was when the raconteur liked to hold court, admittedly to a diminishing number of friends, but occasionally the likes of Sigrid and others kept him company.

Reciting long passages of the classics at any given moment, such as Shakespearean sonnets or Goethe's *Faust*, David never ceased to amaze Sigrid or anyone else who bore witness to his talents. Anything could prompt such a rendition, which could be brief or elaborate. For example, when the topic turned to the influence of the media on the forthcoming election between the two opposing political leaders who seemed to represent similar policies. After indulging in a certain amount of libation,

David was fired into oration, 'Yes, indeed, when the press predicts who will win the election, the troops will follow that trend, "The masses are only moved by things en masse…", as proclaimed by the Director in *Faust*.'

Among his circle of erudites, feisty Stephan ministered the church across the road and occasionally dropped in to join David for a little Scotch or two before dinner. They would discuss issues such as the changes that had taken place in the Catholic Church over the years since both were young. Being brought up as a Catholic, David was endowed with a keen understanding of religious doctrines, which did not mean that he opposed other beliefs.

He hotly debated atheistic views with Dimitry and always felt invigorated after these discussions, which were no doubt fuelled by the Italian white wine both enjoyed.

David's stoic acquaintance Werner, a man of few words, visited now and again. He would play his latest Bach CDs for David, elucidate the finer details in the compositions of fugues to then settle back and listen. David met Werner through one of *Apricity's* fundraising events. Werner's wife, Eva, like David's friend Rose, was a committee member. Having struck an instant rapport, David and Werner became friends. Werner, being quite partial to a *Jägermeister* on the rocks, had introduced David to this chocolate-brown liquid. Occasionally, he brought a bottle along, savouring a couple of glasses with David, then left the bottle, 'Till next time, my friend.'

David liked Sigrid's visits. He enjoyed challenges and reading German was such. His knowledge of grammar often astounded Sigrid and she felt tested when he knew, or recognised, certain German words by the shared Anglo-Saxon root. As a classical scholar, David's vast knowledge of not only German, French, Latin and Greek, but music, history, and many other topics held Sigrid spellbound. He had written seven science fiction novels and corresponded with the American author Ursula Le Guin, pointing out her inconsistencies, which did not seem to lessen their friendly rapport.

Steering the car around the corner, Sigrid now stopped at David's house opposite a church. Overgrown weeds intermingled with remnants of things planted long ago. A pink flowering frangipani had uprooted some palings of the white fence. Tripping through the vegetation, she followed the small winding pavers to the low-set red brick house. She rang the bell, 'Hello, David. How are you today?'

David greeted Sigrid with a continental kiss on each cheek, 'Ah, I'm well, thanks, Sigrid. But I didn't sleep so well last night.'

'I'm sorry to hear that. Hopefully, you'll sleep better tonight.'

'After my daily five o'clock ritual, I'm bound to.'

The two friends paused in the front room. The house's construction had been untouched since the 1970s. It was, to use real estate vernacular, *original*. Bookcases filled the walls and framed the fireplace, in front of which stood, for reasons known only to David, a Besser block embedded with a sword. Every room (and she never did find out how many rooms the house had) was filled with bookcases. But then, that is what you would expect from a literary man of David's age.

In the early days of their friendship, David took Sigrid up to his 'observatory.' The long passage from the middle to the rear of his house led to a roof deck overlooking uninhibited foliage otherwise known as jungle. The smallest of step ladders led up a wall onto the top above one room. The deck was no more than four by four metres. Years ago, David had carefully drawn squares indicating the four cardinal points onto the small linoleum-lined floor. This design seemed to have assisted him in following and calculating the position of the stars. It made perfect sense to David, the astronomer, and he explained it to Sigrid in detail. Alas, she never understood, always attaining a glazed look of polite ennui. However, she admired the night sky and the gradual appearance of all the twinkling stars with him. It was a magical moment, worthy of the precarious climb up, and of course, down again.

Following an established routine, they now settled in the second room to the right, in olive-green authentic Danish lounge-style chairs. On this day of her visit, they started their reading session with chapter twenty-three of *Deutschland. Ein Wintermärchen,* each taking turns to read three stanzas and then discuss the whole chapter. David shared an affinity with the German writer Heine, who, apart from being a Francophile, peppered his writing with wit and political observation. David combined his love for French and German with elan.

Mozart was another passion they shared. After finishing the reading of Emanuel Schikaneder's libretto to Mozart's *The Magic Flute*, they watched a DVD of the 1971 Hamburg State Opera production with Dietrich Fischer-Diskau in the role of the Speaker. As David no longer drove his car, Sigrid would pick him up to play the DVD at her cottage. He appreciated her efforts and reciprocated by inviting her for dinner at the *Amphora*, a cosy little restaurant three blocks away. As usual, he would be in his element, debating and reciting. A different female friend was invited, sometimes even two. That is how Sigrid met *bon vivant* Rose. A vegetarian in her late seventies, delicate, almost birdlike, perfectly coiffured, manicured and Botoxed to the max, with a shrewd mind that David adored. Rose's philanthropy included sitting on several charity boards and being a committee member of *Apricity*. This organisation raised funds for the city's major hospital into melanoma research. Rose generously supported their efforts, after losing her husband to that cancer.

Back in the second room to the right, comfortable in the olive-green authentic Danish lounge-style chairs, they were still discussing Heinrich Heine. Having moved geographically from Germany's winter tale to Heine's thoughts about issues relating to America, David proclaimed,

'"The worldly benefit is their actual religion, and money is their god, their only, almighty god. Does today's religion consist in the monetisation of God or in the godhood of money?" Thus wrote the great literary critic in 1830. And what has changed, Sigrid. What have we, as a society, learned?'

'In that respect, not much, I guess.'

'Complacency, Sigrid. Complacency. We let it happen. And we are complicit.'

'Yeah, well, I think you might be right, David.' Sigrid took a lungful of air, 'Anyway, I've got to pick up my granddaughter. So, I best be on my way.'

Sigrid gathered her belongings and left David with a kiss on the cheek, 'See you next time.'

'I look forward to it. As always, my dear.'

Sigrid trod cautiously along the precarious path in his unkempt and overgrown garden while trying to balance on the small pavers. Opening the car door, she felt relief at leaving. While she valued visiting David, she was now ready for Isabella's company.

Katrina and Peter

Katrina relished having the house to herself. That is not to say that she did not miss her daughter Isabella, but it is nice just to laze about and have some quality 'me' time. For one thing, even though it was late afternoon everything was still as pleasantly clean and neat as it had been when she tidied up in the morning. Peter always left for work very early. Those precious few 'solo' days would soon be gone. She had a chance to do mundane but necessary jobs like clean out the kitchen cupboards, a task long overdue but planned for today. First, she put on Queen's *Greatest Hits* CD, set the ceiling fan on 'high', and with the latest *Vogue* magazine in tow, nestled into her Adirondack chair on the big verandah. The humidity was unusually high and after five years, she still hadn't gotten used to it.

Katrina's hope to return to Brisbane was just not feasible now. The scope and working conditions of Peter's employer in Gladstone, a corporate group associated with producing aluminium, were too good to ignore, particularly with the company's expansion into the global export market. Whichever way you looked at it, and despite what influenced Katrina's opinion about preserving pristine natural resources with her environmentally-focused professional background, being part of a billion-dollar pioneering venture brought a lot of financial rewards.

On the downside, Peter did work long hours and left it mainly to Katrina to bring up Bella. It was Katrina's job to look after home and hearth, deal with *tradies* and generally fix what needed fixing. For instance, she would tear out her hair while liaising with real estate agents about their property down south.

Oh, how she would love to travel like Mother did and, one day, she would do just that. But Peter enjoyed shorter trips to Fiji, Vanuatu, or New Zealand, close to the eastern coastline and not too far away. She contemplated that Bella finished high school in no time at all, and the two of them might just go together. Why not? It was food for thought.

Best to see what Bella's impressions of Germany will be after her trip there. Katrina languidly studied the super-glossy pages of beautiful clothes and makeup.

After a doze, she woke to find it was almost time to get dinner ready. No cleaning out cupboards today, she thought, and proceeded to get her ingredients. She seasoned the veal and sliced mushrooms, shallots, and garlic. Peter was unusually late. His predictable, 'Hi babe, what's for dinner?' made her forget it was already six-fifteen. She asked instead, 'How was your day?'

'Oh, the usual, just another "unexpected" incident that only your hon can fix.'

'Can't they get somebody else to fix it?'

'No, darl, that's why they pay me the money they do. And that's how we can afford to send our princess on a school trip to your mother's old country.'

'Yeah, whatever. Anyway, I spoke with Bella this morning. She seems to be having a good time. Mum is going out of her way to make it nice for her. Although this morning she left Bella at the museum and went to see David, that old friend of hers. I don't know what she does with him. He's pretty old and eccentric from what I can make out, but they meet every week.'

'Ah well, if it pleases your mother, let her be. It gives her something to do. You mightn't like it if you had to look after her all the time.'

'Oh, I know,' agreed Katrina, 'I didn't mean it that way, but you know what I mean.'

43

'Well, we should do everything to support her while she has the energy and capacity to keep herself busy and look after herself. But you know, she's not getting any younger.'

'Nor are we,' exclaimed Katrina, 'and that's why I'd love for us to go on a holiday to Europe sooner rather than later.'

'Oh, here we go again, Katrina. You know that I can't get away for long periods. When you are on a contract, you can't afford to take too much time off. And we had agreed to do this for a few more years while the money's good.'

They were getting close to arguing about an issue discussed many times. While Katrina agreed to the plan of staying in Gladstone to earn the good money, she couldn't help speaking her mind. It all seemed too difficult at times, especially after two glasses of that crisp dry *Santa Margherita* Pino Grigio. Admittedly, moving back to the city now with a nine to five, five day-a-week job would upset everything they had done so far and reduce their income drastically. She might have to go back to work, that is if she were able to get any. On top of it, Bella was quite settled, and it would not be wise to take her out of her class now. By the end of the year, she'll only have a few more years to finish school and Katrina knew how quickly that would pass. She had another sip and a mouthful of scaloppini and thought it best to chew rather than talk.

As if to diffuse the somewhat subdued atmosphere, Peter flicked through his CD's and chose Ella Fitzgerald singing, *It's Wonderful*. Into this musical background,

Peter said, 'Tell ya what, I've got this weekend off. Why don't we drive down, spend a night over the old girl's place and bring Bella home on Sunday arvo? We should be able to manage each way in six hours.'

Katrina was perplexed. This was totally unexpected. Isabella was supposed to fly home Sunday afternoon. But there was enough time to easily change this arrangement. *Why not, why not indeedy?* Her adventurous spirit livened up.

'Now, that's really *wonderful,* let's do it. The change will be good, and I'll get to see Mother.' Inhaling deeply, she continued, 'There is also that place halfway down the coast at Hervey Bay. You know, I bought a ring there, the one with a dark-blue pearl. I wouldn't mind checking out the shop to see if they have matching earrings.'

Peter didn't particularly get excited about that aspect of the trip, but he was pleased it took the sulkiness out of her disposition. He got up, threw three ice blocks into a tumbler, and poured himself a stiff *Jägermeister,* returned to the table and studied the now satisfied features of his wife.

'Um, this does the trick,' Peter said, licking his lips.

'Sometimes, I wish Mother had never introduced you to this stuff in the green bottle. You took to it like a duck to water.'

'Well, she is your mother, and while I don't agree with most of her green arguments, for once, she has won me over with her notion about herbs being beneficial in this concoction. What does she say? "You drink it on any occasion, but mainly for good health." I drink to that. Prost.'

'Yeah, whatever.'

3. Germany 1943–1945

Emilie, Sigrid, Heinz

In Berlin, the situation for Emilie and Sigrid had become increasingly untenable. During the battles in November 1943, thousands of Berliners lost their lives. Constant air raids with heavy bombing destroyed the city and residential areas. The number of homeless people rose daily. To be closer to Heinz and away from Berlin, Emilie planned to move to her sister Rosemarie's apartment in Schwerin, one of the few cities left unscathed by bombing. Exchanging her food vouchers, Emilie managed to get regional railway tickets up to Grabow, halfway to Schwerin. In Grabow, she would have to wait for tickets to become available to continue the journey.

At the beginning of December, the day before a targeted attack caused extensive damage to the Berlin railway station, Emilie departed with Sigrid. Accepting the uprooted circumstances, her young daughter was not questioning only stating, 'Mutti, I am so tired. And I am cold and hungry.'

'Tomorrow will be better, *mein Liebchen*. You wait and see.'

Sigrid yawned, edged into the train's wooden bench, and curled into Emilie's lap.

Shaken in a never-ending manner, they arrived in Grabow. Emilie had been given the name of Dr Willy Havemann. She found his house easily.

'Good afternoon. My friend Jutta Kremer sends us.'

'Ah, yes. Come in. You must be exhausted.'

'This town is like a fairytale. After leaving the ruins of Berlin, I can't see any damage here. The buildings are standing. No broken windows, or holes in walls, or roofs that have collapsed. I can't believe it's still possible to see a place that the war hasn't touched.'

'Yes, we have been lucky—so far. During times like these, you are better off away from the big city.'

Dr Havemann reached for one of Emilie's battered valises.

'We have a spare room for you two. It used to be a storeroom, but at least you'll be safe, and we have blankets to keep you warm.'

'You are very kind, thank you. I hope we will be able to move onto Schwerin soon. My sister lives there.'

'Transportation could be a problem. But we will work something out for you. For now, make yourselves comfortable here.'

The Grabow Sweets Factory was still able to produce some of their famous *Brezel*, *Pfeffernüsse*, and waffles. As it was before Christmas, Emilie was able to get work kneading dough and earning some ration stamps. Frau Havemann looked after Sigrid. Transport proved to be sporadic and stalling. Fortunately, Emilie's income paid for shelter and the next part of the journey. As a keen and able worker, she kept this job till the following summer of 1944, when she finally managed to get train tickets to Schwerin.

Amongst many other passengers, Sigrid and her mother arrived on the train from Grabow without too many interruptions. People were pushing and shoving to get away, out through the tunnel to the front of the Schwerin railway station building. Sigrid and Emilie were swept into the human wave reaching the spot where Aunt Rosemarie was standing on a bench at the end of the platform. She waved excitedly. They were barely able to exchange words. By the time they reached the building's exit, Sigrid had been squashed and trodden on. If it hadn't been for the excitement of seeing her auntie, Sigrid would have burst into tears.

Once outside the railway building, people dispersed onto the station square. Rosemarie embraced her sister and young niece.

'Siggi, how you have grown. Last time I saw you, you were this little.' She pointed down to her knee. 'Let me give you another big hug.'

Rosemarie bent down and squeezed the small girl almost in the same manner she had been subjected to only a few moments earlier by the human traffic. Sigrid was undecided whether to cry or laugh. There is only so much squashing a tiny person can take.

'Let me take one of your suitcases Emilie, and let's get out of this mess as fast as we can.' Rosemarie picked up the other suitcase and led the way through the mayhem, trying to get to their destination in the quickest way. With one hand, Sigrid hung onto her mother, and with the other to her suitcase.

The three of them reached the end of the square and followed the main street for about four blocks, then took a side road and entered Sandstrasse on the right where Rosemarie lived. Her apartment was in a three-storey building. They dragged the suitcases up the stairs, all three levels until they finally reached the tenement in the attic.

'What have you got in that suitcase, Emmi, bricks or a lump of gold?'

'No, Rosie, just some basic clothing, and with winter coming, some are a bit heavy, I guess,' Emilie answered apologetically.

'Never mind, we've made it. Welcome to Rosie's shelter.' She indicated with her right arm, 'Through the hallway into the living room and kitchen. To the right, you'll find the sewing room with two camp beds. To the left is my bedroom. The bathroom is next to it. You can leave your coats here on the rack. Why don't you freshen up while I take your suitcases to your room?'

Turning, Rosemarie added, 'How about a slice of bread with nice thick onion lard for you two bedraggled dears? And a cup of coffee made from some real beans?'

'Oh, Rosie, that would be special. There was very little food back in Berlin. People were trading their precious heirlooms for such basic things as eggs, butter, bacon and milk. They do this even in Grabow.' Emilie gasped, 'And it will be good for Sigrid. She needs wholesome nourishment to grow. Her legs are a bit bent. You can't really see it through those trousers, but she is suffering from rickets.'

Emilie effused, 'I know we are going into winter, but surely here in Schwerin the sun will be brighter, the sky will be bluer and the food more nourishing. I'm just happy and thankful that you have taken us in, my dearest. Also, Heinz is not too far away. His *HJ* camp in Malchin is really just a short distance from here.'

'Maybe we can ride a bicycle to see him. That would be so nice,' interrupted Sigrid.

Emilie's cheeks flushed with increasing excitement, 'It will also be good for little Siggi to see her brother more often.'

'I am not little. My birthday is soon, and then I will be seven years old.' Sigrid objected.

Rosemarie cajoled, 'Of course, you're not little. You are my big little niece, aren't you, dear?'

'Yes, but not little anymore,' Sigrid sulked.

'As far as the sun and blue sky are concerned, Em, the sky darkens here too, you know.'

Bending towards Sigrid while caressing her right cheek, 'And you, *mein Liebes,* Malchin is near but not near enough to ride a bicycle. Also, I'm not sure how the *HJ* would welcome a visit from family at the camp. Anyway, you must be starving. I'll get on with the food while you two wash your hands and settle in.'

Emilie and Sigrid unpacked their few belongings and put them into the small chest of drawers Rosemarie had emptied.

'Mutti, did you see the colourful fans and shawls that Auntie Rosie has hanging on the walls in the living room?'

'Yes, I did. Your auntie is a dancer in the ballet at the State Theatre. Before the war, she worked for Circus Busch and was on tour. She used to travel quite a bit. She even went to Holland and Italy.' Pointing to a framed photograph on top of the chest of drawers, Emilie continued: 'See, that's your auntie when she first started to dance.'

'Oh, she is beautiful. I'd like to be a dancer,' Siggi swooned with passion.

'When this war is over, we'll talk about it. In the meantime, we better fatten you up a bit and make sure your legs straighten enough for you to dance.'

For some time, life was quite idyllic for Sigrid and her mother at Aunt Rosemarie's. Because of her night work at the theatre, Auntie had to sleep in and Siggi tried to be noiseless in the mornings. The highlight in Sigrid's recollection was her brother Heinz's surprise visit for her birthday in September. The day had started routinely: a quiet breakfast with Mother, followed by playing in the inner courtyard with her new friend, Monika. In the afternoon, Sigrid drew, looked at pictures in the books from Aunt Rosie's bookshelf or observed the birds hopping around the ashen boughs in front of the attic window. Sometimes she watched her auntie put on makeup before it was time for Siggi to set the table for dinner. Mother was assigned to work in the aircraft components factory during the day. But this day was different.

Mother came home in the early afternoon. Sigrid was sent to the neighbour across the road to pick up some mending, with which Rosemarie earned a few *Reichsmark*. When she returned with the sewing, Sigrid felt a little excited. After all, it was her birthday and Mother was home already. But nothing had prepared Siggi for what she saw when she walked through the front door.

There stood Heinz, her big brother. He was very tall and tanned. He looked smart in his dark long trousers and shirt, his shiny belt buckle, and boots. Most of all, she liked his big grin and the mischievous twinkle in his eyes.

'Hey, little sis, happy birthday. You didn't think I'd let the occasion of your seventh birthday go by without a fuss, hey?'

Heinz picked up Sigrid and swung her around the room, nearly knocking over the chairs around the table. He recollected how much he had missed his sister, who was growing up all too fast.

'Oh, Heini, I'm so happy you are here. How did you get here? How long will you stay?'

'I caught the train via Bützow. I've got to be back the day after tomorrow. I was pretty lucky I could get away;

Uncle Adolf doesn't like us to spend too much time away, if any,' emphasising the noun, 'time, with our families. It interferes with and influences our training.'

'You want to be careful how you talk about the *Führer*. Any sense of disrespect is not tolerated, as you should know by now,' Mother admonished.

Not fully comprehending this moment of gravity, Sigrid said with passion, 'I wish I could come with you.'

'You're still a bit too young. Wait till you grow up more and everything else will follow.'

Heinz held out a small item, 'Look what I've got for you. I made it myself.' He put a little package in Sigrid's hands.

'What is it?'

'You'll find out when you open it.'

Sigrid unwrapped the wax paper, which revealed a small squirrel carved from light-brown linden timber. Stroking the curves, she exclaimed, 'Oh, that is so beautiful. I love it, thank you. How did you know I like squirrels? I've seen some in the woods here. Look, Mutti and Auntie Rosie, isn't it lovely, just like we saw the other day? I'll call it *Knusperchen* (little nibbler), and I'll take it with me everywhere.'

'It will remind you of your big brother, who looks after you. Always remember that.' Heinz said with conviction. But then he wondered how he could look after her in these turbulent times, not knowing where he might be stationed next. At least for now he was not too far away.

'Alright, now have a look at that, big Siggi.' Aunt Rosie led everybody to the table which was set with red bows placed around a *Gugelhupf* (buttercake), on top of which were seven lit candles. Sigrid stood in wonder and after a while mused, 'Ah, that is lovely. This is the best birthday ever.'

'Hold on a minute. I just want to take a photo of you behind the cake, Siggi. And then one of you with Mutti and Aunt Rosie.' Heinz proceeded to snap away and concluded his task with, 'There's bound to be a good one between these shots.'

'Wait, not so hasty. Let me take one of you with Siggi and Mutti.' Rosemarie took the camera off Heinz and started to click, click and wind several times. 'Okay, and for good measure, just one more of only you two *Lieben*. Put the knife into the cake and cut it.'

'That's a bit big for you, Siggi. Let me help you with the cake.'

Heinz gently put his right hand over Siggi's arm to hold the knife. After all this excitement, they sat down and enjoyed the cake. Emilie did not really want to know how Rosemarie managed to get hold of the ingredients. Various mysterious goings-on occurred but sometimes it was best not to know too much, especially in circumstances where an oppressive regime rules with a ruthless fist. These days Emilie lived very much by the principle 'Just be quiet and hope it will get better.' Besides, she was more than grateful for the shelter and generous hospitality her sister extended to her and her children. It was hard enough with their father being in action on the Eastern Front.

Just before Mutti switched off the light, Heinz poked his head through the doorway, 'Sleep well, Little, umm, Big Sis, and tomorrow I'll take you out in a boat on the lake around the castle of Schwerin. You never know what fishy creatures might pop up. Good night.' He gently closed the door.

It had been a big day for Siggi. So much had happened since 1943; *Pappi being away from home, Heini going away and coming home and going away again. Mutti and me moving from Berlin, then being squeezed into the little room at Grabow, the ride in that horrible, overcrowded train, and now living in one room at auntie's in Schwerin. At least the bombers did not drop bombs here every night. They just flew over on to Berlin and made enough noise doing so. Also, we do not have to run into the air-raid shelter every night.* Now she could get some sleep. She touched Knusperchen. Knowing that her big brother was just behind the door gave her the comfort to doze off into sleepy land.

The next morning promised a reasonable autumn day and while the sky was overcast, the cold of winter had not yet set in. After breakfast, Heinz and Siggi set out with a basket containing a few lard-spread bread slices and a thermos flask of tea and a sheet of sailcloth to sit on. They walked down to the lake, through the old cobblestone streets with their grey truss houses, past the baker's elegant wrought iron guild sign hanging on the corner of the baker's shop. Schweriner Sea was edged by fog.

Heinz managed to organise the hire of a rowing boat. At almost fourteen years of age, he was the big brother who took care of things. Siggi had been in a boat on Berlin's Wannsee when she was little but could barely remember it. She wasn't really scared; it was just very wobbly to get into.

Rowing on the Schwerin Lake

Once settled, Heinz skillfully rowed across the lake. The water was still. Siggi followed the wave pattern generated by the oars, and every now and again, fish created a slight movement in the distance across the water. Gradually the haze lifted. Siggi saw the castle appear right in front of her. What a sight, like a story out of her *Grimm Brothers'* fairytale book.

The castle, that had stood there for many centuries, rose majestically from the misty lake against the greyish-blue sky. The rectangular five-storeyed shape was surmounted by four prominent slate-coloured towers on each corner, a golden onion-domed roof and a slender dark grey spire. A number of larger and smaller towers took up the space between the four main ones. In the middle of the front wing stood the statue of a rider on a horse, the Obotrite Prince Niklot, who back in 973 built a Polabian Slav fort on this site. The castle, built on an island, was connected to the land by a bridge.

Schwerin Castle

'Oh, Heini, that is just beautiful. I saw the castle when I went with Mutti to Auntie Rosie's theatre, but I've never seen it from the lake. Can we get closer to it?'

'Just watch which direction I'm rowing in, and you'll see we're getting closer.'

Heinz rowed steadily towards the castle until the building with its big towers disappeared behind the trees. They entered a huge artificial grotto made from large boulders. When they got close, Heinz fastened the boat's rope through an iron ring hanging from one of its pillars. The floor of the grotto was gravel. The water lapped gently against the bottom of the boat. Heinz jumped barefoot into the water and held his hand out to Siggi, 'Come on, step onto the edge of the boat, and I'll carry you across to the pebbles.'

After Sigrid stepped onto the stones, she excitedly ran to the end of the grotto. When she turned around, she could see Heinz's silhouette contrasting against the shiny silvery sea behind him. He picked up the basket, and they walked through the low rock-lined ceiling and narrow passages of the grotto's innumerable columns.

'This is a bit scary, Heini.'

'Don't be scared, I'm with you.' Heinz said reassuringly as he gently put his arm around her. Siggi remembered the last time Heini had said that. It was after Father was drafted and after Heinz was sent to Berchtesgaden and came home again.

I never forget it. I'd been playing hopscotch with the kids from Schrammstrasse. It was great playing in the rubble in the side street's courtyard. An older boy found a rope and tied it around the arch of a huge hole in one side of the wall. We took turns to swing backwards and forwards. It was so much fun. When it was my turn again, I grabbed the rope and was ready to lift myself up when Heinz appeared suddenly. He ripped me away from the wall and bent over me, shouting to the others, 'Get away. Get out. Get OUT.'

Crash! The bridge of the wall broke. Dust and bricks flew into the air and spewed onto the ground. A piece of brick scraped my leg. It started to bleed.

'This place is dangerous.' Heinz yelled. 'Never play in ruins again, Siggi. Those bricks could've buried you.' His voice broke. 'Lucky, I got hold of you before…'

Heinz wrapped his arms around me. He wiped my tears away with the sleeve of his shirt and pressed a hankie onto my leg. Cuddled me. I felt warm and safe.

From inside the grotto, the sight was rather eerie, a dark hole from which a narrow tunnel led out onto the lake. Siggi followed Heinz confidently, and after they had reached the last arch, they stepped onto the browning autumn grass that edged the island.

'Let's find a place where we can have our food.'

Nodding, Siggi trailed close behind. They walked along the edge of the Orangerie building until they found a spot near the water.

'This will do, don't you think?' Heinz asked.

He spread out the sailcloth and placed the basket in the middle. 'Sit down and let's have something to eat.' Heinz handed Siggi a doubled-up slice of bread and then proceeded to bite a chunk out of his own. They sat in silence, chewing and soaking up the tranquil yet strangely unnatural setting.

If only life could always be this peaceful. Heinz contemplated. *You could almost forget that cities are being bombed and more and more men will never return home.*

During Heinz's short life, he had not experienced too much tranquillity. Since his early years, political fanaticism had encircled his normally pacifist household and the spread of the National Socialist oppression had affected the most apolitical of households. When he was ten years old, Heinz had to join the German Young People (*DJV*) as a cub. That was the beginning of his political indoctrination, regimentation and discipline. Then Father was drafted to serve on the front, and Heinz was sent to Berchtesgaden. Now he was allocated to the Hitler Youth Malchin Regiment. He was fortunate that the under fifteen-year-old group leader (*JSF*) gave him permission to visit his mother for his sister's birthday. He had witnessed instances where those in charge had not been so obliging and denied similar requests from other cubs. By now he had made up his mind not to ask for any more favours. It did not endear him to the other boys. Best to enjoy today with his little sister. Tomorrow morning, he had to be back in Malchin. At least he had a friend in Werner there.

Rising out of his brooding, Heinz said, 'Come. Come, I'll show you something.'

On the water's edge, he gathered a handful of smooth flat black pebbles, and gave one to his sister. 'Watch what I do,' he said as he threw one stone to skim across the water, letting it skip six times.

'How did you do that? I want to do it too.'

'Ok, throw it quite low and close over the water like this.' Heinz responded as he threw another pebble. But Sigrid's stone thudded sluggishly into the lake.

'Keep trying. You'll get there.'

It took more than several attempts, but eventually Sigrid managed to have the pebble jump the water twice. She felt satisfied and quite proud that her brother had taught her how to master the art of pebble throwing. As they returned to their spot on the grass, Heinz asserted, 'I've got another surprise for you. Let's put the basket back into the boat, and then I'll take you to see some of the museum's staterooms inside the castle.'

'Oh, really? Are we allowed to go inside?'

'Yep, we are. This will be something you'll remember forever. Your brother taking you inside a real castle.'

Indeed, Sigrid did, especially as it was to be their last outing together. In future years she remembered visiting the huge regal room with the throne at the end topped by a rich burgundy and gold velvet canopy. The ceiling centrepiece surrounding the chandelier consisted of beautiful paintings and the whole marble-columned room was covered in portraits of people and angels. Throughout her life, she would not encounter a sight like that again, certainly not in Australia.

'Oh Heini, this is a real fairytale castle.'

'Yep, it is, I've got to say. Let's move on.'

Siggi's recollection of the other halls morphed into rooms full of paintings, statues and ornaments. But two pieces were to remain prominently on her mind. The first was the statue of the palace ghost *Petermännchen,* who, dressed in a seventeenth-century costume, stood with his legs apart, both arms bent and each hand holding a long stick. He had a defiant look, a frilled neck roll and a huge hat with a feather plume. She felt both attracted to, and scared of, this tiny character.

Petermännchen

Observing her fascination prompted Heinz to assert, 'This little fellow is supposed to haunt the castle.'

'Oh, really,' Siggi replied, somewhat hesitantly.

'Yes, but don't you worry too much. According to legend, he lives in the vault. He rewards honest people and chases the baddies away with his sticks. And, because you are such a goodie, you'll be safe.'

She grinned and hugged him.

The other item she remembered was the beautiful porcelain figure of a lady sitting on a chair. She wore a voluminous yellow dress with blue trimming while a kneeling cavalier kissed her left hand. She looked happy and carefree. 'One day, I'll be a dancer too, like this one and like Auntie Rosie.'

'You never know what might happen, little one. Remember, if you think you should do something that you really truly like, do it. You've got my blessing.'

That comforted Siggi. She felt so lucky to have a brother such as Heinz. Not like her friend Monika, whose forever uniformed brother Siegfried told authorities everything she did and everything her mother said. He always searched Monika's room, and if she had anything that he considered to be unfavourable to the *NS* regime, he'd simply destroy it.

Monika had treasured a postcard depicting a little girl with a dove. She found it in the abandoned apartment of the Meyer family and showed it to Siggi a few times. This postcard was of a Pablo Picasso painting, not that she knew who that was. Monika particularly liked the way the little girl cradled the dove with such a contented yet longing expression. How was Monika to know that Picasso was an enemy of the great German state, and his works, like that of many other modern artists, were branded as degenerate art? Just like the book burning orgy in 1933, these paintings were destroyed in a bonfire in 1939. By then, many artists had fled into exile if they had the means. As a result of their perceived threat to German culture, Siegfried tore Monika's favourite postcard into many little pieces, shaped it into a mound and set a match to it.

No, Siggi's brother would never do such a thing. He was a good person. She could talk to him, and he would always take care of her.

The next morning when Siggi woke, Heinz was packed and ready to head back to Malchin. 'My train goes in one and a half hours. Do you want to come to the station?'

'Yes, yes, I want to come. Wait for me to get dressed and then we'll go.'

'No, no. No rush. There's enough time for you to have some breakfast. Auntie Rosie has managed to get a few slices of salami.'

They sat down together and even though the aroma tempted Siggi's nostrils, she was too restless and choked to eat.

'Come on, at least have a bite for your big brother,' Heinz coaxed. Siggi forced down the prized food.

'There you are. Have a sip of coffee and then another bite. It's already easier, isn't it?'

After a silence, Heinz, holding something mid-air, teased, 'I've got a present for you.' He handed Siggi a photo showing the two of them in front of the birthday cake from the day before. 'Oh, that's wonderful. When did you develop that? Auntie Rosie only took it yesterday.'

Sigrid's seventh birthday with Heinz

'Big brother doesn't muck around little sis. I did it last night while you were in slumberland. That's why I've lugged my development gear all the ninety-five kilometres to Schwerin and will lug it all the way back to Malchin in this big rucksack. Of course, you didn't see me arrive. Otherwise, you would've noticed.'

'Ah, I had to go on an errand when you got here. But I'll go with you to the station now.'

Siggi picked up the photo and studied it. Heinz stood behind her. His left shoulder was slightly turned, cradling Siggi as if to keep a protective shield over her. He held her left arm in a guiding manner. Both were smiling happily. The harmonious bond between the two siblings was evident, prompting Siggi to say, 'It's really special. Thank you so much, Heinz. I'll always treasure it.'

'Well, keep it somewhere safe. It's me looking after you even when I'm not with you,' affirmed a slightly emotional Heinz. Pulling himself together, he continued, 'Ok, let's go then.'

They walked along Sandstrasse quietly, onto the square in front of the railway station from where they went through the tunnel to Platform Three. Since this train went on to Berlin, many civilians and returning soldiers were already queuing to board the train. It puffed slowly towards the metal buffer at the end of the track. Passengers climbed up the steep steel grids and disappeared inside the carriages.

Heinz lifted Siggi, hugging her against his chest in an intense embrace, 'Bye, Siggi, look after yourself and Mutti.' As if to divert the emotion of the moment, he added, 'I'll carve you a little mouse and post it to you. And I'll also carve you a frame for the photo.'

'Bye, Heini,' is all Siggi could get out of her clamped throat. Her eyes welled up as Heinz clambered up the stairs to the train. Instead of wiping away her tears, she took out her handkerchief and waved towards the spot where Heinz had disappeared. Perhaps she had a foreboding that she would never see her beloved brother again.

Heinz and Werner

The cold of an early November winter in 1944 arrived in the township of Malchin overnight. Autumn had stripped the trees of their leaves. An icy wind was blowing through the narrow alleyways. Even the old red bricks of the gothic town gate had taken on a pale hue. The water tower stood above the faded, ochre-roofed houses of the town's centre. The lakes of Malchin and Kummerow reflected the grey sky. East of Malchin Lake stood the fourteenth-century castle Basedow, one of the biggest castles in the north of Germany and the proud ancestral seat of the Hahn peerage.

The apparatus of Hitler's Youth Realm Directorate (*RJF*) had occupied part of the original village grounds that surrounded the castle. The vast expanse of the once-stately park created by nineteenth-century artist gardener Peter Joseph Lenné had been converted into a Third Reich learning institution. Its organisational centre was a low set rectangular red brick building with a gabled roof that was one and a half times the area of the building, typical for this region. The pitch-roofed entrance was positioned in the middle of two sixteen-windowed blocks. The Hitler Youth national school administrative centre occupied the right wing. The class and activity rooms and dormitories for the ten to fourteen-year-old boys (*DJV*) were to the left.

These boys were grouped into five categories. Curricula was based on subjects including military, naval, sport, administrative and general fields. They practised close-order drills, infantry tactics, camouflage, marksmanship, and hurling hand grenades. Proficiency and leadership qualities were deemed to be of utmost importance. The enormous grounds surrounding the building were ideally suited for the physical part of training. Overall, the primary purpose of this extremely well-organised apparatus was to recruit, indoctrinate and prepare a junior army replacement pool. They were to be obedient, savage warriors for their *Führer* and the Third Reich. This consortium was to be physically and mentally equipped to defend the Nazi regime against anticipated enemies.

It was in spring, eight months earlier during one of their plotting-the-enemy-position-with-map-and-compass drills, where Heinz met Werner. Not yet thirteen, Werner had survived the death of his family. Because of his brightness, he was advanced into the German youth folk unit (*JB*). He mastered scheduled tests with excellent results and participated in all the exercises and tasks.

When not taking part in regimented and structured activities, this lanky brown-haired boy was inclined to keep to himself as much as possible. Werner wandered through the woods in the neighbourhood, lay under one of the old oak trees or sat on the lake's edge and read classics like Schiller's *The Robbers* or Charles Dickens's *David Copperfield*. But he also read the *Kampfblatt* (Fighting paper) which the *NSDAP* regime tailored to brainwash and prepare Germany's population for political initiatives and forceful intervention. These activities occupied young Werner's life until he encountered Heinz, to whom he was intuitively drawn.

Their friendship was based on a mutual appreciation of sport and nature. They also had a competitive streak and took turns in coming first in the sixty-metres running race and long jumps. Moreover, both detested the compulsive gossip of the boys who spied on others and then informed the German youth folk leader (*JB*).

Heinz questioned Hitler's indoctrination which was unusual in this milieu. His younger friend Werner, due to the loss of parental guidance, and an absent relationship with the world outside the regime, was more susceptible to the ideological training and adherence to his cub oath—to be faithfully obedient to the *Führer*. Werner wore his 'Blood and Honour' inscribed dagger with pride. He had been schooled from a young age by Nazi teachers along the lines of one of the Jesuit maxims, 'Give me the child for the first seven years, and I'll give you the man.' It was believed that those being indoctrinated for political fervour would achieve positions of leadership which were useful to the command.

Out of respect, the two boys had a silent agreement not to deliberate on their ideological divergences. Whenever they could get away from the regime's structured curricula and the noise of the other boys, they would, depending on the season, enjoy indoor or outdoor activities. In winter, they spent time developing the films they had taken during their outings in the frosty surroundings. They sat in front of a fire whittling ornaments from wood. During summer, they hiked in the woods, swam in the lake, or rode their bicycles. On one such day in June, they rode their bikes north past the township of Malchin onto the nearby remains of Remplin's castle park.

The exquisite charm of the many hamlets in Mecklenburg often led to this area being referred to as German Switzerland. It still concealed numerous castles of former dukedoms. Count Friedrich II. von Hahn from another branch of the Hahn lineage of nobles had built the first star observatory of Northern Germany on his estate in Remplin in the late 1700s. The moon's crater 'Mare Hahn' was named after him, in recognition of his work in astronomy.

As the boys cycled along the tree-studded park lane, they reached a lake in front of them. It was with great surprise that they set eyes on the reflection of a domed tower in the water.

'Is that what I think it is?' Heinz blurted out.

Werner answered, 'Looks like an observatory,' adding, 'That?—in the middle of nowhere?'

'Only one way to find out. Let's head towards it.'

They rode their bikes closer, marvelling at the grey tube-shaped construction, hinting at its former splendour. The tower was approximately fourteen metres high and topped by a smaller level, crowned by a grey dome. A steel staircase wound itself along the oblong windows of the first floor and the arches of the second, up to the top lookout.

Before they could put down their bikes, Heinz called out, 'Come on, a race to the top.'

Werner just beat Heinz, and once they reached the platform, Heinz gasped, 'Wow, look at that; that's better than the view out of the oak trees in the forest near the estate.'

'Sure is,' was Werner's pensive reply.

Remplin Observatory

The many tinges of lush green went all the way to the pale blue horizon before them on the right. On the other side, a few hundred metres away, a line of treetops covered an alley made up of hundred-year-old linden trees leading towards the lone medieval gate tower. Apart from the north wing, this was the sole surviving relic of the once-baronial Remplin castle, destroyed by a fire in 1940. Besides the observatory, a creek ran into the small viridescent lake. A narrow-arched footbridge made of roughly hewn boulders crossed the creek. Meadows, bushes and different types of trees were spread throughout. The whole vista was a carpet of diverse levels and shades of green set against the pastel sky. A slight breeze wafted around them.

'I'm glad we took this track. Let's keep it to ourselves. The others can find out for themselves if they want to.'

'Yep,' Werner answered.

The two boys sat in silence on the floor of the lookout, their legs dangling through the railing. The stillness of the moment, accompanied only by the wind whispering through the trees and the faint chirping of birds in the distance, had a profound effect on them. For a while, their world was beautifully and peacefully theirs. Each lingered in his own memories of some good moments' past.

However, a distant but distinct hum of artillery drills from Basedow base brought the youngsters back to reality. This prompted Heinz to suggest, 'Let's go for a swim and then head back before somebody reports us missing, eh?'

'Yep.'

After their dip, they agreed that this was one of the best days of their lives. 'Yes, it was very special. I'll always remember it,' confirmed a normally reserved Werner.

After Heinz's return from visiting his mother and sister in Schwerin, the cooler autumn weather set in swiftly. The boys displayed a keen interest in photography, a pastime encouraged by the regime. As Werner had his father's Brownie Six-20, and Heinz his Agfa Synchro Box, they took many snaps of their surroundings. These shots could be of the bark of trees, creatures in the grass, the ruins of the castle and occasionally, each other.

One day, they cycled to the observatory to capture the magic of their earlier summer excursion. Heinz took a photo of Werner on the spiral staircase of the observatory.

'Wait there. I'll set the timer and we'll get a shot of us together.' Heinz rushed to Werner's side.

How different this moment was. The overcast sky accentuated the dreary atmosphere. It's doom and gloom were aptly reflected in the dark and grey tones of the tree trunks, the murky lake and creek.

As Heinz already knew how to develop films, he instructed Werner in the procedure and the necessary steps to process his own photographs. When Werner hung up his roll of film from the observatory, he caught sight of Heinz's already dried roll, 'Is this when you went to Schwerin to visit your mother?'

'Yeah. Which one are you looking at?'

'That one of you and the girl behind the cake.'

'Ah, that's my little sis. Siggi. It was her birthday.'

'She reminds me a bit of my sister,' Werner choked. He turned and crept outside. The pain of hearing that his mother and sister had perished in the shelter during the air raid in Hamburg was still too fresh in his mind. As he was heading towards the woods, he heard steps behind him.

'Come on, man, I know you're hurting.' Heinz embraced Werner and patted him on the shoulder. The young men hugged in silence.

'Hey, what's going on with you two?' bellicose Herbert shouted.

'Look at them. Sissies, and they're supposed to fight for the *Führer* and the Fatherland,' yelled Hartmut.

'*Schwule, Schwule* (homos),' cried another three boys who appeared from nowhere.

'Stupid idiots. Do ya want a fight? Piss off before I get stuck into you. You stupid idiots.'

Heinz's face was red, and he was ready to punch anybody who came too close.

By now, Werner was sufficiently provoked to swing into a boxing position with his fists clenched. The wild determination on the two friends' faces and their unflinching body language diffused the tenseness of the situation, causing the other boys to lay off. Brushing off this encounter, 'those fools are not worth it,' Heinz tapped Werner's shoulder and they headed back to the darkroom.

Another of their common pursuits was the building of a crystal set. Werner managed to smuggle some crystal set parts from his training session. The boys took great care not to be discovered and derived satisfaction with their achievements.

However, in late October, Werner was assigned to the Hitler Youth signal training (*HJS*). The aim was to prepare him for duty in the signal units of the Hitler Youth News Service. His training included an introduction to communication procedures, the operation of simple signal instruments and equipment, and morse code.

At the beginning of his training Werner still saw Heinz. Eventually, Werner became increasingly involved in his specialised signals training and with the passing of time, they saw each other less frequently. What's more, in a reversal of roles, it was Heinz, who was keeping to himself and now the loner.

Towards war's end

A great fire broke out during the winter of 1944/45, destroying much of Basedow castle. One of the flying embers sparked the stables adjoining the Third Reich learning institution. There were no casualties, but the damage was such that all Hitler Youth cubs had to be accommodated elsewhere. Heinz was sent to a school camp in Neustadt, north-east of Lübeck.

Werner, because of his outstanding academic grades, was promoted to go to the secondary school (*RHS*) in Heiligendamm. The boys said their goodbyes with some sadness. Their rapport and respect for each other had not waned.

In Schwerin at the end of 1944, all theatres closed, Rosemarie lost her job. Swamped by refugees, deportees and fleeing soldiers, she considered the town unsafe and decided to make her way to Frankfurt. Emilie had also been able to leave Schwerin with Sigrid before the take-over by Allied forces. Taking great risks and evading the almost continuous bombing by British and US air forces, they somehow managed to get through the bedlam to Göttingen where they sheltered with Emilie's friend Gudrun. Eventually, that town was annexed to the authorities of the British occupation zone and became part of West Germany.

The winter of 1945 was harsh with heavy snowfalls. Since January, Germans from East Prussia were leaving their homes and farms en masse. They were running away to the West to escape the Russian Red Army advancing from the East. These evacuees put their most precious belongings and whatever else fitted onto their horse-drawn carts and tracked westwards through deep snow. During the night, the sky behind them in the east was as red as blood from the fires of townships. At times, the refugees got caught in the path of the retreating German military for whom they had to move aside. Overtaking numerous wounded German soldiers, the diverse group of landowners, aristocrats and workers schlepped their gear, while deserters and escaping war prisoners moved amongst them.

Caught between the Russians behind them and their own army in front, the evacuees lost most of their meagre possessions, and in the end, just tried to move to the West. Those, injured or frail, were left behind.

During the following months, as the snow was beginning to melt, wagons stood up to their axles in mud, and dead horses exposed remnants of their once bloated bellies. The muddied tracks kept the Russians at bay for just a little longer while the refugees tried to put as much distance between them as their cold and tired feet and their weary bodies and minds could manage.

In early April, some of the displaced persons passed through Malchin. They were still heading west and trying to evade the Red Army, who, by the end of the month, occupied the severely destroyed township.

In the meantime, the Eastern Demarcation Line was divided between the Anglo-American troops and the Red Army. This line ran from Schwerin up to Wismar on the East Sea. In May, American troops took Schwerin. They turned the city over to the British, who then handed the command to the Soviet forces. In due course, Schwerin was to become part of communist East Germany.

Werner spent only a few months in the secondary school of Heiligendamm, the former white 'Dame' by the sea. Set now against the achromatic January sky, the original beauty of this grand hotel was still evident even though in

1943, Nazi cadets had moved into its once glorious main building and replaced the lavish furnishings with ordinary office fixtures. A couple of years later, refugees from Pomerania and Silesia fled the Russian army and took refuge there.

Werner's schooling took place in House 'Doberan.' This was located halfway between Heiligendamm and Bad Doberan, which was infamously the first town to appoint Hitler as an honorary citizen; a bestowal, embarrassingly still in place in 2006, a few months before the G8 summit in Heiligendamm.

As the 1945 Wismar Demarcation Line was approximately forty kilometres from Heiligendamm, Werner's class was relocated to a school camp in Neustadt in April. In a desperate attempt to salvage whatever possible for the *Führer*, the obsessive battalion leader subjected the boys in his care to intense indoctrination. Mantras drummed into the boys were: 'A soldier who defends just one square metre of ground, defends Germany,' and 'Our squad only knows one rule—to strive forward—to turn back means death.' As part of their military and ideological training, leadership was stressed equally with ability and fervour in attack and weaponry.

The boys, amongst whom thirteen-year-old Werner was by far the youngest, were ready to fight for their Fatherland. They were part of the territorial army of young boys and old men (*VS*) raised towards the end of the war to obey the Nero Decree to defend and fight for the Third Reich to the last man standing. Equipped with anti-tank guns, anti-rocket launchers, armour fists, steel-hand grenades, guns, pistols and in some instances farmers' forks, they were programmed to fight to their death. This motley, and at times fanatical bunch, persecuted and murdered real or suspected regime opponents in the name of the *Führer*.

Neustadt was overrun by refugees, transports for the wounded, deserters, people fleeing from the bombing of Hamburg, lost soldiers, and released inmates of Neuengamme concentration camp. This resulted in a chaotic accumulation of humanity.

Heinz's death

Heinz had been in Neustadt since December 1944. His schooling took place on the outskirts of the town. Thus, contrary to Werner's regiment, which inculcated German orderliness and punctuality, Heinz's school had given way to the general confusion that reigned the last months before the war's end. Covertly sharing Heinz's Nazi dislike, his teacher, Herr Rindermann, turned a blind eye to Heinz's escapades to the township. He was rarely reprimanded for his sporadic school attendance. In between helping civilians clear the rubble, Heinz often lingered at the harbour, hoping to catch sight of Werner, as he had heard of his friend's transfer. Heinz was looking forward to seeing Werner again, hoping not to have to post his letter with a photo from Remplin Observatory.

While the Russians were advancing from the East, the Eleventh Armoured Division of the British forces had crossed the river Elbe in the West, occupied Lübeck and then moved onto Neustadt on the third of May. This was a particularly nice day in spring. Anticipating an end to the horrors of war, Heinz and a group of other disillusioned boys were lingering on the east side of Neustadt which was connected to the west side by a bridge. As SS snipers were still active in the town, the youngsters learnt to be cautious and were hiding in a ditch near the crossing of Schiffbrücke and Brückstraße. They wanted to be the first to greet the British Black Bulls, now considered as liberators in this region.

Across the bridge, the comet tanks approached with incessant thudding. With all eyes set on the tanks, nobody noticed another group of boys joining the cluster. The first tank reached the bridge's east side when Heinz perceived Werner's frame to his right. *I don't believe it. It's Werner. Here. Next to me.*

Turning intuitively, Heinz rose to greet his friend.

In a split second, he realised that Werner, focusing on the first British tank, raised his right hand, clenching the wooden handle of a *Stielhandgranate*.

'What are you doing, man?'

Oh, no, not Heinz. Not now. I got to fulfil my mission.

A wrestle ensued. Heinz instinctively tried to seize the handle of the steel hand grenade. He eventually succeeded by hurling it into the empty field behind them. The sound of an explosion penetrated the zone. Thick dust engulfed all.

Wiping off the dirt, the once best friends stood face to face; querying and speechless. The sound of a single shot from close range was barely audible. Heinz coughed, 'That was close.' He turned his head from side to side and looked at Werner, stupefied, 'Don't you know? We've lost. The war is over. Man.'

Grimacing in pain, Heinz clutched his chest and slumped onto the rubble. Propped up on his left elbow, he stared in disbelief into Werner's face. Slowly but incessantly, the blood trickled out of the corner of Heinz's parted lips, as he exhaled, '*Du Idiot*.'

Instantly, Werner understood that he had lost his only friend. He bent over Heinz, cradling his head and torso. He studied the features of his friend. Heinz, who had extended his friendship to him. Heinz, who made the unbearability of having lost his family bearable. Heinz, with whom the moments in Basedow represented flashes from a world buried in his early childhood memories. His friend, who had taught him that there are moments of beauty in darkness. Who had introduced him to the art of capturing precious moments on film. Heinz, who had lost his life because of him.

The Nazi regime's methods of indoctrination produced exemplary results in Werner's intended act. He was defending his *Führer*, to whom he had sworn allegiance, obedience and action with 'Blood and Honour.' Werner's judgment had lost clarity. The battalion leader in Doberan, had he not disappeared after the last training session, would have reaped the benefits of his intensified fanaticism planted into Werner's orphaned young mind.

Heinz's last words were to haunt Werner for the rest of his life. If only he hadn't blindly followed the battalion leader's instructions on that fateful day on the third of May 1945, so close to the war's end.

If only—how many times are these two words uttered? Probably seldom with the immense regret he felt. He could not help his father's death, nor his mother's, nor Anna's. But he could have prevented his best friend's.

Boys, British soldiers, and civilians rushed in from all directions. A buzz of activities ensued. The teacher, Herr Rindermann, emerged from the gathering crowd. Bending over Heinz, he asked, 'What happened? Why? Why Heinz?'

Werner stammered that Heinz was his best friend. That Heinz tried to wrestle the hand grenade off him and that he, Werner, was the cause of this tragedy. Herr Rindermann pushed Werner away. He felt for Heinz's pulse and put his ear next to Heinz's mouth. Pressing his lips together, he gravely shook his head. After a pause, he talked to other boys, and they removed Heinz's body.

Herr Rindermann, tired after years of war, was frustrated by fanatical bureaucracy. He was sick through malnutrition, disillusioned after losing most of his family, friends and colleagues. He wanted to put all those nefarious years of terror behind him and simply return to his fishing shack on the island of Rügen. All he wanted was to put a stop to all this horror and madness. Madness that had killed millions of people, injured and maimed, caused people to go missing, be misplaced, leaving chaos and destruction. The teacher always liked Heinz. Dead now, because of his indoctrinated friend, who, after all, was only thirteen. He seemed remorseful and understood the magnitude of his erroneous action. May he have a new start, if that is possible. All considered, he was an ill-advised youth and seemed to be smart enough to have learned his lesson.

Werner's cohort surrounded him, commiserating, 'Oh, that could've been me.' Werner's head pounded. He had to get away. He pushed through the youngsters and ran, just ran until he collapsed somewhere in the ruins.

The British version of the incident was that a fanatical Hitler Youth member tried to attack the first of their tanks by throwing a hand grenade. In the ensuing commotion, eighteen-year-old foot soldier Frederik Winsall, walking alongside the tank, instinctively reacted and fatally shot the youngster. The incident was brushed off like others, as an act by an extremist German prepared to fight until the very end.

At school camp Herr Rindermann gathered Heinz's belongings: an Agfa Synchro Box camera; a *David Copperfield* book, 1920 edition, a wooden carved photo frame; an unsealed letter with a photo of Heinz and that boy in front of an observatory, addressed to Werner Müller, c/o Otto Müller in Hamburg. The teacher bundled up Heinz's possessions. He packaged the items and agonised how to inform Heinz's mother. He eventually sent a letter to Frau Emilie Hermes, c/o Gudrun Moltke in Gőttingen, saying how sad he was to have to tell her of her son's involvement in an accidental and fatal shooting during an attempted last-minute attack on the liberating forces. He emphasised his impression of Heinz having been a 'fine young man' and listed the burial site.

Herr Rindermann also forwarded Heinz's letter and the photo to Hamburg.

On the day that Heinz lost his life, one of the largest maritime losses took place near Neustadt. The Royal Air Force bombed every ship along the coast trying to stop fleeing German officers and soldiers from getting to Denmark. They sunk the prison ship *Cap Arcona*. Onboard, destined for Norway, were about five-thousand prisoners from Nazi concentration camps. German trawlers rescued some crew members and guards, but most of the prisoners were refused embarkation and left to drown. Those concentration camp detainees who managed to swim ashore in Neustadt were mercilessly gunned down by SS disciples.

The last short and yet painfully fatal moments before Germany's inevitable capitulation bore witness to far too many evil deeds committed by members of a population who were hopelessly misled and susceptible to malevolent actions.

During the downfall of the Third Reich, the battalion leader, responsible for Werner's unwarranted action, was not the only militant group member to behave with inhumanity. Right until the collapse of the Nazi regime, cities like Schwerin had some factions of the party who continued to keep hundreds of concentration camp deportees in pitiful conditions under guard with dogs.

Finally, the news spread that Hitler had died. On hearing this, the local teacher Marianne Grunthal called out with relief, 'Thank God, then this terrible war will be over at last.' This was overheard by SS guards who hanged Marianne on the second of May in Schwerin's Central Station Square. It was only hours before American troops arrived. That square was since named in memory of Marianne Grunthal as a reminder to never again succumb to those atrocious deeds. Humanity can only affect change by remembering. But—have these lessons been learned?

The unconditional surrender of the German armed forces on the eighth of May ended World War II. On the fifth of June 1945, the Allies' unilateral declaration broadcast their supreme authority over Germany. The country was now occupied and governed by the four Allied forces: the United States, Britain, France and the Soviet Union. They divided Germany into the capitalist West and the communist East. Berlin, isolated like an island in communist Germany, was divided into four zones. It was not until the twelfth of September 1990 that the foreign ministers of the four occupiers signed a treaty to grant a united West and East Germany full sovereignty.

4. Australia 2013

Sigrid and Isabella

After leaving David, Sigrid drove back to the museum to pick up her granddaughter. The road along the river was relatively traffic-free. Moving towards the bridge, Sigrid turned right, then left into the gallery precinct. Isabella was already waiting in the area designated for buses and taxis.

'Hi, Oma, that was good timing. I only just got out of the building,' Isabella effervesced as she slipped into the passenger seat.

'I'm glad it worked out so well, Isabella. Did you find what you were looking for?'

'Yes. And not only what I was looking for, but so much more. It's such an amazing place. I wish we could have a museum like that back in Gladstone. My friends would love it. It's awesome. *The Hidden Treasure* exhibition is amazing.'

She opened a page in her sketchbook, 'Look here. I've sketched the most beautiful belt from it. It's gold. It is so intricate and delicate, just as I drew it. I've got so much material for an assignment on ancient Afghanistan. You know, it was once on the crossroads between the Silk Road and the nucleus of activities. Such as,' she hesitated, then continued using her fingers to enumerate, 'cultural, artistic and economic. It's just so interesting, Oma. We could both see the exhibition for a second time. I don't mind going again, in fact I'd love to.'

'Well, it was on my list of things to do while you're visiting. I just thought I should check first. Remember when I used to get tickets for the ballet before you and your mother came down?' She continued in a lower tone and obviously peeved, 'Then I found out that other plans had already been made.'

Missing the innuendo, Isabella chatted with fervency all the way home and Sigrid was quite happy to listen; it gave her a chance to change her disposition after her session of stimulating discourse with David.

The phone rang as they entered the cottage.

'Do you want me to get it, Oma?'

'Yes, please, you're faster.'

Isabella spoke for a while before handing the phone to Sigrid, 'Hi Mum, how's it going?' asked Katrina.

Sigrid had hardly answered when Katrina blurted out, 'Guess what, Peter has this weekend off, so we've decided to come down and pick up Bella, if that's ok with you?'

'Of course, Trina, that will be lovely. You know I've always got a bed for my favourite people. Isabella and I will be ready for your visit. Won't we, Isabella?' she voiced over her left shoulder towards the direction of her granddaughter. Mother and daughter chatted for some time, sharing the latest news and events.

'Well, I better hang up now, seeing that we'll be together in a couple of days. Isabella must be starving and, so am I. Till Saturday afternoon darling, or whenever you get here.'

Grandmother and granddaughter sat down to a late lunch consisting of a cob of corn and salad.

'I might go for a dip in half an hour. It's warm enough now. What've you got planned for the afternoon, Oma?'

'Well, I had my swim this morning. You know my routine of fifty laps, fifty scissor jumps, fifty hip rolls and fifty other things.'

'Hmm.'

'I think I might give Kylie a workout.'

'Kylie? Ky-lie?'

'Well, you see, I've got this gentleman friend Alistair. He absolutely adores Kylie Minogue. Mind you, he could be her granddad. But that doesn't stop him from raving on about her. He claims to love her. Though obviously not enough to spend four hundred dollars to buy a ticket to see her perform at a live concert. At least I love Gerard Depardieu enough to spend twelve dollars fifty to buy a movie ticket or thirty-eight dollars for a DVD.'

'Uhh, yuck, fat and big-nosed Depardieu,' interjected Bella. 'You still carry on about him?'

'He wasn't always like that, you know. He was very handsome in his younger years and he's a great actor.' Slightly piqued she pointed her nose up into the air, scantly shook her head from right to left and continued, 'You only have to see him in Bertolucci's film *1900*.' She paused briefly, 'Anyway, Alistair happened to visit one day when the robotic vacuum cleaner was delivered. So, he helped me set it up and promised to come back to watch it work after it was fully charged. The next day we got it going, and it rushed ahead with full force. It just so happened that the ABC played an orchestral version of Kylie's *I Should Be So Lucky*, which prompted Alistair to burst out, "Why don't you just call it Kylie?" Well, why not, indeed? So, we named the vacuum Kylie.'

'Ah, that's sort of funny, Oma. Can I see how she works?'

'Sure, but it's a bit of an ordeal. You see, first, I've got to get rid of all the rugs. Otherwise, she gets entangled in the fringes. Then I've got to move the small tables. Otherwise, she gets caught in the legs. Then I've got to move the Berliner chair because the frame makes it difficult for her to move over and out. Then I've got to block off the bedroom and my study.' She took a deep breath and added, 'There are just too many obstacles that might entrap her.'

Not noticing Isabella's disappearance, she continued animatedly, 'I always start her in the bathroom where I lock her in after I moved the scales, laundry basket and rubbish bin off the floor. Then I put her to work in the kitchen, where I run a race with her and my dustpan with which I sweep the fluff and crumbs out of corners and crevices where Kylie can't reach. So, you see…where, where are YOU?'

Turning towards the verandah, following Isabella and not missing a beat, 'Anyway, it's quite an ordeal. You may ask, why bother? Well, she does a good job, if only to get me motivated to move the furniture and start on a house clean. Otherwise, it might never get done.'

By now, Isabella was very sorry she had asked. Her desire to see Kylie in action had well and truly dissipated.

But Oma continued, 'There is something funny I have to tell you. Last time Alistair was here, I couldn't get Kylie to start. So, as soon as I let him through the door, I said, "Kylie has died." "Oh no," he said, seriously distressed. You know, of course, why he was distressed?'

'Not really, nooo.'

'He thought of Kylie Minogue. Poor chap. Anyway, when he found out that it was only robo-Kylie, he was obviously relieved and switched her on without any probs.'

'What was the problem?' Isabella inquired lamely.

'Oh, there is an on and off button that needed to be switched on.' Sigrid answered sheepishly.

'Oh, Oma, you are funny. Well, a bit.'

Raising her eyes upwards, Sigrid responded, 'Yes, I know, darling. A few friends have told me that I'm a bit funny.'

Rose

Bon vivant Rose lived in a penthouse apartment on the river at St Lucia and, amongst other things, divided her time between seeing her gentlemen friends Alan, Rupert, and Judge James. She met them respectively for lunch in the city on Mondays, Wednesdays and Fridays. Not necessarily each week, but certainly on a regular basis.

How she fitted David in was a bit of a mystery, but fit him in she did, regularly on Tuesdays and Thursdays. David was her favourite, as he was privileged to see Rose twice a week. She was amusing, kept the conversation going and was popular. No doubt, her quick-witted sense of humour and her outspokenness about any topic at all had something to do with it. Widow of a renowned English surgeon, Australian-born Rose, who lived in England for many years, held on to a more British accent than the British. Whether, it was in dedication to a husband, dead for some years, or as a means of making a statement, was unclear. To emphasise a point, and disregarding the social etiquette to remember names, she would address those with whom she was currently engaged, as 'sweetie this' and 'sweetie that.' This characteristic, as well as fascinating episodes from her life, lived well, resonated in the ears of her entourage for many years.

Early Wednesday Rose sat on the enormous balcony of her penthouse, still enjoying the aftertaste of her coffee and croissant. The brown river glistened in the morning sun. The reflection of the trees in the park on the opposite side cast long-serrated shadows to the middle of the fast-flowing water. She observed a hive of activities in the parkland. There were joggers, people walking their dogs, mothers and some fathers pushing prams, and a few 'oldies' (who were usually younger than Rose) sitting on the benches reading a paper or a book. She was pleased to see this type of pastime. Rose did not favour the now usual human trait that she observed in cafés, restaurants, taxis or indeed anywhere at all, of people glued to their i-phones or umbilically attached to their tablets. She was determined never to have anything to do with this type of technology. She did not use the internet, did not do emails, or 'sweetie forbid,' did not use Facebook, Twitter, or Instagram, whatever they were.

Face to face contact was Rose's preferred means of communication, and the telephone was, and would forever be, her second favoured modus operandi. And it did ring quite frequently. Rose was popular and, being generous, made her acquaintance even more attractive.

Thanks to regular cosmetic procedures and touch-ups, her mask-like, but by no means displeasing face, exposed hardly any wrinkles. Her weekly visits to Cameron, who knew how to keep her well-groomed without altering too much of her basic chignon style, assisted in enhancing her attractiveness. Her silver hair had a hint of pink, purple, dark blue, metallic grey or even corn gold, depending on which of her gentlemen friends she cherished on a certain day of the week. For example, when meeting with Judge James, her hair was tinted in sophisticated grey to enhance the dusky pink of her Chanel suit. Reassured by this attire, she put forth her notion about 'the intolerable situation of only summoning unemployed people for jury duty,' a sentiment strongly repudiated by the Judge.

Apart from her regular luncheon engagements, Rose had a busy week ahead. She expected her daughter Alexandra to ring from London with the updated details of her planned trip to Brisbane. Not that it involved any work on Rose's behalf, Alex was well organised and always stayed at *The Chancellor,* but nonetheless it would occupy her thoughts for a while. Since John's death, Rose had returned to Australia, but Alex built a 'wonderful' career with a television studio in London and preferred to stay in the country of her birth.

Jo, the help who came five mornings a week, appeared on the balcony to remove the Villeroy and Boch china. 'Is there anything else I can get you, Rose?' she enquired.

'Ah, yes, sweetie, would you mind calling me a taxi, please? To arrive in half an hour and to take me to Park Road in Milton. And just carry on with whatever you are doing now. Thanks, sweetie.'

Rose got up and walked along the mirrored corridor to her somewhat dated *Sex-in-the-City*-inspired walk-in wardrobe. How she had enjoyed that show, watching it with Fleur and the other girls while sipping a little Moet in her sumptuous living room. Yes, the series was a bit silly but enormously amusing, nonetheless. Her assessing glance registered the hanging suits. She decided that a trouser suit would be fitting for the occasion. Navy with a white shirt. You can never go wrong with a white shirt.

This week the colour of her suit would complement her dark blue hair. She changed from her kimono into her chosen outfit, put on her navy platform heels, and picked up the same-coloured small Gucci clutch.

She stopped in front of her full-length mirror. Her right hand stroked her chignon approvingly. She powdered her nose and applied a pink-tinged lipstick. Notwithstanding that, in this age of cosmetic enhancements, a person's age was not always easy to gauge; she felt inclined to consider herself in her early sixties. Thus, her figure was erect, her gait straight and her appearance exuded triple capital Cs– Classy, Cheeky, and Cheery. She approached her front door, 'I'll see you tomorrow, Jo,' and left the penthouse.

Downstairs, the taxi was already waiting, and so it should. The ride to Park Road took less than five minutes and she felt pleased to be on time for once. Inside *Apricity's* boardroom, most of the committee members were already seated, although a few were still busying themselves with coffee and biscuits. Rose positioned herself between Roger, the chairman and Eva, the secretary, and settled down as comfortably as she could in one of 'those' office chairs.

'It is 10:00 am, and I declare the meeting open,' Roger announced. Rose absented her mind from the mundane business of the minutes of the last meeting, the treasurer's report, and correspondence. But when Roger raised the topic of fundraising, it sparked Rose's interest.

'The university's research team at the hospital has worked very hard. Very hard indeed, facilitating a range of not only research projects but clinical trials. Imagine using immunotherapy to stop the melanoma metastasing. This project looks excitingly promising. It will fulfil their mission of zero deaths from that disease.'

'Agreed. Quite so.'

Riding on the wave of general sanguinity, Roger continued, 'It will, of that I am quite confident, save many lives in the future.'

'Hear, hear.'

'And that is why, as a supporting organisation, we should raise more funds to help continue with this, not only worthwhile but lifesaving research.'

'Agreed. Indeed.'

'I am very happy to host a fundraising event at my penthouse.' Rose's highly anticipated proposition was warmly received, and approved by the meeting, which Eva duly noted in the minutes. Rose knew how to throw a party; the committee was united in their appreciation of that. With Rose's social connections, it was bound to be another profit-yielding event for that all-important research.

The committee settled for the fifth of October, enough time for publicity yet not too far away; conveniently close to the holiday season and yet sufficiently distant from the first Christmas engagements. With this strategy, they felt good attendance numbers and profits for the organisation would be assured. The meeting closed at 11:47 am, and the members proceeded to leave the building. Eva stopped Rose at the elevator, 'Rose, would you like some help organising anything for the function?'

'Sure. If you want to look after the invitations and name tags, I would appreciate that. As far as catering is concerned, once you have definite numbers, just let me know. I shall get my caterer Hugo to whip up something. As you know, sweetie, he is absolutely wonderful. Takes care of everything, simply everything: canapés, mains, desserts, drinks, waiting staff; the lot. I only employ him. He never lets me down. If you want to know a secret, Eva, he is the reason my functions are so successful. Got to fly now. Ciao, sweetie. We'll keep in touch.'

Rose floated out of the lift, down the stairs of the building and across the road to her, not normally scheduled, luncheon with David in *Café de Paris*. David was already seated. He stood the moment Rose swept through the swinging doors.

Rose and David

David enjoyed Rose's panache. It reminded him a little of his youth in Calcutta, white-gloved ladies with white sun umbrellas, delicately embroidered, drinking gin with lime from long glasses and, like Rose—utterly stylish.

'Good afternoon, Rose. You are looking as splendid as ever.'

'Oh, thank you, David. I do like your bow tie, the paisley pattern is ever so refreshing. What shall we eat? I am dying for a drink, sweetie.'

'The bottle of Moet should be here any moment. I know how you love it.'

'Guess what, sweetie? I am having a fundraising event for *Apricity* on Saturday, the fifth of October. You'll be there, darling?'

'Saturday? The fifth? Well, I don't believe that I am doing anything, but I'll check my social calendar,' he replied with the slightest touch of sarcasm. They often played their little games, Rose being the social butterfly and David, the inveterate hermit.

'Monsieur, your bottle of Moet et Chandon, *si'l vous plait.*'

'Yes, fine, thanks. Start pouring, please,' David beamed.

'Cheers, sweetie.' Rose took a long sip out of the champagne flute. 'I shall never tire of these bubbles. I feel like Madame Bollinger. I shall drink this nectar when I'm happy, when I'm sad, when I'm alone, and when I'm not. I'll drink it when I'm hungry and when I'm not and I never drink it unless I'm thirsty. And this, sweetie, I happen to be all the time. Cheers.'

'Oh, Rose, you are incorrigible, but I love you, dear. Cheers.'

The two perused the menu and ordered garlic bread and a light salad. David visited Rose usually in her apartment, but this was one of those occasions when they met for lunch at a restaurant. During the last six months, it occurred a few times after Rose's meetings at *Apricity*. The building accommodating this charity was right in the middle of the restaurant precinct of Park Road, very convenient and most conducive to Rose's habit of restaurant lunching.

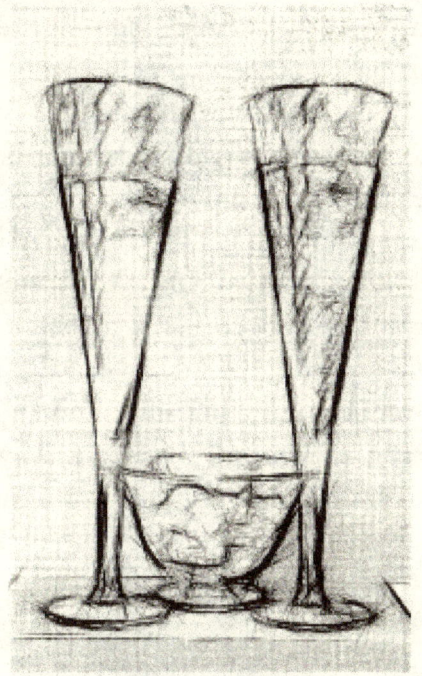

Cheers. Sweetie.

Discussing the latest news, it was Rose who now filled in David with what was happening in the world, as he seemed preoccupied with his *belles-lettres*. Yet, Rose too had a keen understanding of literature. Indeed, they initially met at one of his former U3A classes. But today, it was the Prime Minister's sacking, that had Rose all fired up.

'Love her or hate her, sweetie, it is abominable what the media and her party did to her. She never had a chance. Even though she held the numbers initially, thrashed out one policy after another through the House, and created a world sensation with her speech on misogyny. The constant nasty personal attacks and white-anting did not cease until the moment they succeeded with her removal as PM. It makes me want to go back to England, sweetie.'

'Yes, I did follow some of that on the ABC News, but why go back to England? It's the same there as it is here. In fact, if you think about it, it's the same all over the world,' David replied. 'And I do agree, what they did was detestable. But people are not silly. You know. They are aware of what is happening.'

'Alright, sweetie. Have it your way. Anyway, we'll find out soon enough. The election is just a few weeks away.'

Several weeks later, Rose and David sat on her balcony. She sipped on her flute of bubbly. The setting sun filtered through the foliage and buildings across the ink-black river. Two CityCat ferries passed in opposite directions, each leaving a white foamy trail. Some of the clouds in the sky had a purple-bluish tinge around the edges, a forerunner of the rising moon.

'Another Scotch, sweetie?'

'I'll get it dear,' David replied as he got up to make his way into the kitchen.

He returned, 'Life's jolly good, dear,' and settled into the deck chair while raising his glass, 'Cheers.'

'Cheers, and yes, it's pretty good, though I must admit organising the fundraiser has kept me on my toes more than I had planned. And it isn't over yet!'

'Can I be of any assistance?'

'No. Thanks, sweetie. It's all under control. Hugo's staff will serve cocktails on arrival and then a continuous array of finger foods, wine, beer, champers. Later there'll be petit fours with coffee. Numbers are really good. A few people have enquired if they can bring family members. Sigrid is having her daughter and son-in-law stay overnight. You know my attitude, sweetie. The more, the merrier. And it's all for such a good cause.'

'Yes, it is. I must admit I do like catching up with most of them. I don't really get around that much anymore and, as you know, I have given up on having people over for meals. Just a drink with nibbles now and then is all I desire.'

'That reminds me, Jo left a platter of olives, cheeses, bikkies, nuts and dates in the fridge. Would you mind getting it, sweetie? I've got napkins on the table here.'

David got up and did as he was told. He did not really mind. In fact, he quite enjoyed being bossed around by Rose. 'That looks delicious and very appetizing. You've got a gem in Jo.'

'Yes, I know,' Rose replied. But don't put the platter straight onto the table. There's a place mat for it to sit on.

'Here's to tomorrow evening, my dear. Success, fine wine, delicious food, interesting friends and a lot of money for your *Apricity.*'

'I'll definitely drink to that, sweetie!' After a moment of silence, Rose continued, 'Now that the election is over, people will be more generous with their donations tomorrow. It's peculiar really, as if the outcome would affect their spending that much. People will still have their Moet, their Audi and their holiday unit down the coast. They'll go on their overseas vacations and send their children to private schools.'

'No, not everybody, you know. Not all are as fortunate as you, dear.'

'I know, sweetie, but you get the gist. What really changes for the ordinary citizen?'

'Quite a lot. Ignoring climate change, lack of more investment in renewable energy, leniency towards coal seam gas mining and slower broadband are issues that will eventually affect everyone. If not in this life, then in the lives of those who come after. Not to mention a fairer treatment of indigenous people, people with disabilities and asylum seekers.'

'Yes, yes, you are quite right, of course. But are you so sure that if the others had remained in power, they would have done everything they had promised in the last months before the election? Why didn't they fix at least some of the issues, like the health debacle, for example, when hospital staff did not receive their pay for months on end, and others were paid double? They were in power long enough and had sufficient time to fix it.'

Rose was on a roll but paused to have another sip, giving David the chance to interject, 'Of course, you know, that was a state issue.'

Swallowing, Rose continued, 'Yes, yes, alright, sweetie. Have it your way. But through my other charity work, I have heard of terrible decisions made by young and inexperienced doctors who work in the admissions section of the general hospital. A decision such as sending a mentally unstable young girl with an extremely high blood alcohol level home by taxi – why? Because of a lack of beds. My friend told me that when this girl got home, she jumped off the roof of her apartment block. She's now a paraplegic. Imagine if she had died. Wouldn't the coroner have questioned the doctor's decision? Now we taxpayers must foot the bill for that unfortunate lass. What she needed was a bed, compassion, supervision, and counselling, not a taxi home. In that state, I ask?'

'That is indeed most unfortunate, Rose. And I agree it was a bad decision, and you wonder how these things slip through the system. But the issue is quite complex, dear. A hasty decision or an oversight can result in a mishap. Especially when allegiances are tied to Uncle Sam to such an extent that institutions like our universities, for example, have changed their whole terminology and degree structure to comply with a computer program designed for the American market. And, regarding the state's new computerised hospital payroll system, it did have some glitches. Who knows, was it even designed for the Australian hospital system? That does happen.'

'Well, sweetie, then they shouldn't have released the payroll program until they were sure that it worked to perfection.'

'Yes, I can't argue with that. Still, you've got to look at the overall picture and sometimes you must take the good with the bad and hope that the good outweighs the bad. It is unfortunate for those people who get caught when efficiency has slipped between the cracks. I agree, it should not have happened. The new system should have run parallel to the old, in case of malfunctioning. It should only have been released upon certainty that it worked one hundred percent.'

Both sipped on their respective drinks. By now it was quite dark except for the lights in the apartments and their flickering silhouettes in the moving river. This setting inspired Rose's pondering about her life in London with her husband John and their frequent trips to Florence.

How I savoured the view from the villa in the Tuscan hills over the winding Arno. The Ponte Vecchio in front of the other bridges. The marvels in the Uffizi, with my favourites: Raphael's 'Madonna of the Goldfinch' and Botticelli's 'Primavera.' John's tongue-in-cheek persiflage about the Botticelli depicting a bunch of vestal virgins who celebrated the fruit of their forbidden love. Haha, how they were concerned about the evident consequences of being impregnated. He was so amusing with his humorous commentary how each female found herself in this predicament. This, of course, always involved members of the Medici family and the clergy.

How I miss John's droll thoughts and his companionship. We did have some jolly good years together. But he died far too early. That wretched melanoma took him quite by surprise, really, and then it was simply too late. It had spread throughout his body. If only awareness and today's research had been around then.

She paused for another long sip of bubbles.

At least he didn't suffer too much. Towards the end, Alexandra hardly left his side. She was a great comfort to me in the days that followed. But she has her journalistic career at the TV station in England and I don't see her too often really. And now she's had to cancel her trip. At any rate, while we're separated by distance, at least we ring each other regularly. Indeed, I might phone her tonight.

As she considered this possibility, David stood up. 'Rose, dear, I think I might head off now. Thanks for a pleasant evening and I shall see you tomorrow.'

'I'll see you to the door, sweetie.' They bade each other farewell. David walked the short distance to his house. Rose poured herself another bubbly, nestled down on the couch, forgot about Alex, and switched-on *Miss Fisher's Murder Mysteries*. She watched with glee the glamorous lady detective's fight against crime in 1929 Melbourne.

Katrina and Peter

Back in Gladstone, Peter called down the staircase, 'Are we all packed and ready to go?'

'Yep, I've got my overnighter ready. What's that box in the corner here?' Katrina shouted up the stairs.

'Ah, it's a surprise for Max. I thought he'd like a genuine vintage Brownie Six-20 for his birthday next month. I got it off the net, saves me posting it to him. Tom can hide it till then.'

Checking her fringe in the mirror, she queried, 'Max? Brownie? What twenty?'

'Max. My nephew.' He raised his arms. 'Brownie is an old make of camera. One of the first ones. Back in the day some people developed their own films. In fact, kids did too. If they were faultless and aesthetically pleasing, they got a brownie point.' He burst out laughing.

'Get it?'

'What? Ugh, not another dad joke, and Isabella isn't even here.'

Sighing he continued, 'Oh, anyway, you heard of Leenie Reifensteel, or whatever her name was. The German filmmaker. She was right into it.'

'Oh, no need to tell me. I know all about old photographs. Ever since I can remember, Mother has that sepia photo of her and my uncle, whom I've never met. He developed it himself. You've seen it many times.'

'Yeah, sure. That's what got me interested in the first place. Anyway, it's a bit of an "in" thing at the mo. Boys of Max's age like that sort of thing.'

'Isn't Max too old for that at fourteen? He's into computer games and the latest tech gizmos.'

'I don't think so. Of course, he's into computers as well, that goes without saying. But he seemed interested in having an original Brownie the last time I saw him.'

Peter came down the stairs, picked up the box for his nephew and packed the car for their journey to Brisbane. They swung themselves into their Toyota Sahara Land Cruiser, released the roller door and drove off. Small droplets of water covered the grass, and steam rose from the landscape as the first rays of sunshine made contact.

'I must admit I like early mornings, not that I see them that often,' Katrina said with a yawn.

'Enjoy. It's quite a novelty for you. Not like somebody else, who's out at the crack of dawn, slaving to bring home the bacon.'

'Oh, my poor babe. I so appreciate what you're doing. If you're a real good boy, I'll give you a massage next time I think of it.'

'Story of my life—*next time I think of it.*'

Peter grunted and switched on the radio. Katrina settled back into her seat. In no time at all, Peter could hear her rhythmic breathing. There was hardly any traffic on the road. Peter enjoyed the vastness of the scenery with its rolling hills bordering onto the olive-green mountains in the distance. Dotted throughout was a white farmhouse or homestead usually on top of a hill.

Intermittently, he'd drive through a tiny township and before realising, saw, 'Thank you for visiting Booyal. Have a safe journey.' *Didn't know I'd been there. Hmm, must be time for breakfast.* Katrina was still sound asleep. He decided to stop at Hervey Bay for a bite, nothing too heavy. He should be able to make it in an hour.

Driving along the highway provided a pleasant break from Peter's professional routine. Working in Health and Safety for the alumina refinery meant that he had to be always on alert, especially now they were tying Stage Two into the operational refinery with an anticipated hydrate output of more than double its capacity. The safety of his crew was always on his mind. He dreaded the possibility of having to face a family member with the devastating news of a fatal accident.

Having this weekend away was a rare luxury. He also knew that a long-term career with his company helped build a secure future for his family—a topic needing further discussions. Katrina still believed their stay up in Gladstone was for a limited period. Peter knew only too well that the money he earned there could not easily be achieved in Brisbane, and he wanted to make the most of it for now and beyond. If Isabella started university, she could settle in with her grandmother. They got on well enough. And Katrina, well, if she really wanted, could get a job. She has plenty of friends in Gladstone, and Brisbane is not that far away. Katrina could even go on a trip to Germany with Bella in a few years. But first, it was Bella's turn with her school trip.

'Uh, are we there yet?' Katrina yawned.

'I'm fast, and amazing, but give me a break. We're almost halfway. I'm also starving,' Peter answered.

'Ok, ok, just kidding anyway. Actually, where are we? I wouldn't mind having a bite either. Let's eat something healthy like avocado and a poached egg on yummy sour dough.'

'Your choice, we can either turn off here to go to Hervey Bay or continue onto Maryborough.'

'Well, it's still early enough. Why not go to Hervey Bay and enjoy the early-morning sun on the water.' After a pause, Katrina added, 'I might find the earrings to match my pearl ring. That's if the shop is already open.'

'Ok, Hervey's it is for something healthy.' Peter turned off at Torbanlea. Half an hour later, he parked the car in the street parallel to the ocean. As they got out, Katrina stretched and arched her back, 'Isn't the water beautiful?'

'Sure is, babe.'

All the way to the horizon, light danced amidst the pale blue ocean, and towards shore, the waves rolled in smoothly onto the yellow-brown sand. The slender grey-green casuarinas edged the beach, their branches moving gently and elegantly in the wind.

Peter and Katrina chose a café opposite the water and sat down. The tablecloths were blindingly white in the sunlight. After a quick perusal of the menu, Peter ordered coffees and 'Hervey's Special' consisting of bacon, sausages, tomatoes, mushrooms and two fried eggs. Katrina ordered Eggs Benedict.

'So much for a healthy brekkie, eh?'

'Don't feel guilty, Kato. It's not that often that we hit the long road to Brissy. We deserve a little treat every now and then.'

'Smooth talker, you,' Katrina grinned and with cappuccino froth all over her upper lip, gave him a smack of a kiss.

Katrina did not find the matching earrings for her pearl ring, but she and Peter arrived at her mother's place in Kenmore in the early afternoon.

5. Germany 1945–1965

Emilie and Sigrid

In June 1945, German cities and infrastructure were largely reduced to rubble as a result of the war. Millions of refugees from the East flooded West Germany. Large portions of the population were suffering. They were hungry, broken, disillusioned and had lost their homes and whatever belongings they once owned.

Yet mail delivery did occur, albeit not regularly, and Herr Rindermann's small parcel eventually reached Frau Hermes in Göttingen. Puzzled, and with trepidation, she opened it, 'My son's Agfa camera. A wood-carved photo frame. A book *David Copperfield* dedicated to my son by Werner? A letter from a stranger? Herr Rindermann? What is the meaning of this?' she uttered to herself. With trembling fingers, she opened the letter.

'No, no. Oh, no!' Emilie slid onto the chair.

'My son. My only son. And the war is over—finally. But my son is dead.' *A confrontation. An accident. Fatally shot.* Brokenhearted, Emilie buried her head in her arms on the table. The last decade of pandemonium took its toll, she burst into uncontrollable sobs that shook her slight frame.

After a while, small arms embraced her tentatively. A little head rested gently on her back.

'Oh, Siggi,' Emilie turned. 'My darling. I forgot all about you. Come into Mummy's arms.' Emilie cradled her daughter and slowly calmed herself.

After a while she sat Siggi on her knees and stroked her head.

'Siggi, we won't see Heinz again.' Sensing the enormity of the moment, Siggi did not ask why.

'My dear little girl. Your brother was shot. He is not coming back to us.'

'Not ever?'

'No, not ever.'

'But he promised me that he would always look after me.'

'I'm so sorry,' Emilie's tears streamed down her cheeks again.

'He said he would. Always.'

Heaving with sobs, Emilie enfolded Siggi into her chest. Her young daughter did not understand. 'What about Pappa?'

'When he gets back with us, everything will be better. I promise you.'

Freeing herself from the embrace, Siggi looked into Emilie's eyes. 'Mutti, I don't want to be called Siggi anymore.' Tears were running down the child's face.

Emilie took her daughter's hands and cuddled her ever so gently.

'That's alright. My dear Sigrid. That's alright.'

Emilie knew her son, and even though she had not seen him in the months before this terrible news, she was sure that Heinz had not been part of any antagonistic confrontation with the liberators.

He had too often voiced his scepticism about the *Weltherrschaft* (world domination) doctrine governing the school curricula. Whenever his discussions with Aunt Rosemarie in Schwerin had taken place, it had prompted Emilie to intervene. She dampened their criticism of the Hitler regime. She feared that neighbours might overhear the heated discussions or that Sigrid might inadvertently repeat what she heard at home. There were enough spies around to inform on any political dissent. Those who were denunciated, ended up being accused of high treason. As if the concentration camps were not full enough with people who dared to be different, who were born the 'wrong' race, possessed a personal affliction contrary to the regime and were too outspoken and non-conformist.

Heinz was not a turncoat. He would not have changed his attitude, especially not so close to the end, which was so obvious. This madness could not have continued any longer, not when there were no men left to fight. Those children, hidden in the ruins, amongst the falling bombs, hurling hand grenades at the invaders, were being encouraged and rewarded with bravery decorations by the few remaining Nazi officials. Those youngsters were only being primed to end up as cannon fodder. Emilie knew this only too well, and Heinz was of the same conviction. Her sadness was mixed with anger, but who was there to question, to be held accountable? Emilie's experience with authorities was one of frustration.

She had once gone to the authorities, requesting that her husband should get an additional two weeks leave after returning weakened from the Eastern Front. Instead, he was sent straight back as an act of punishment for her daring to ask. Therefore, Wilhelm had only been home for two weeks. Heinz never got to see his father, as he was in Berchtesgaden during that time. From then on, Emilie avoided having any dealings with officialdom. She would leave it to her husband upon his return to investigate the real circumstances around what happened to their son and the exact events of his death. Now that the war had ended, it would not be long before Wilhelm's release from the prisoner of war camp in the Soviet Union. Then he will get things sorted. They would go back to Berlin and make a fresh start. She and Wilhelm would rebuild the future for Sigrid's sake. She had to comfort her daughter, who still did not seem to comprehend that she would never see her older brother again. The brother who had become her trustworthy father figure.

In July 1946, Emilie and Sigrid eventually managed to find their way from Göttingen to Frankfurt. Emilie did not want to return to Berlin. She had received too much heart-wrenching news. First, the notification that the British Black Bulls accidentally shot Heinz at the end of the war.

As if that was not enough, she then received a letter from the government advising her that Wilhelm died in April 1946 as a result of pneumonia in a prisoner of war camp in Krasno-Uralsk, Russia. He was one of the 542.911 war prisoners to die in USSR captivity from May 1945 till June 1950.

Sigrid did not really absorb this significant news. Barely remembering her father, she had always been closer to Heinz and was still coming to terms with losing him.

Rosemarie had already left for Augsburg in Southern Germany. After a tearful farewell she had followed Neale, an American G.I., who was stationed there.

The journey from Göttingen to Frankfurt was potentially fraught with obstacles. Displaced people were not allowed to go just anywhere. Usually, they were allocated to certain regions, depending on where they came from. Frankfurt, like so many other cities, was severely damaged by bombing. The city was allocated to the American sector, its administration had a reputation of treating German citizens well. This was verified to Emilie through her acquaintance with Neale, whose assistance enabled her and Sigrid to get transport to Frankfurt.

During the early days of the occupation, quite a friendly trade took place between the Germans and the *Amis*, who would swap cigarettes, nylon stockings, chocolates and as an extra, chewing gum, for Nazi paraphernalia like Hitler Youth badges, daggers or uniforms.

Some of the German population were only too happy to get money for their Third Reich belongings. Ironically, but unsurprisingly, as if by a miracle, former Nazis suddenly vanished from the face of the earth the day the Allied forces had determined Germany's political fate. The emerging Nazi material was often from anywhere and anyone but the original owners. Those who profited from racketeering adapted very quickly to ways of reaping benefits from any situation.

Since accommodation was scarce in Frankfurt, Emilie and Sigrid were allocated a small room in Herr and Frau Lindbaum's ground-level apartment in Liliencronstrasse. Contrary to its name, life was not crowned with lilies in Liliencronstrasse. The owners of the apartment, the Lindbaums, were not at all happy having to share. Being Jewish and among the first returning to Germany, Jewish people were given preferential treatment in an embryonic attempt to ease the collective guilt of the German authorities and people. On the one hand, this was the first step in an endeavour to achieve redemption and reconciliation with the victims. On the other, the homeless population needed to be off the streets. This required mandatory measures that were not popular with everybody, as feelings were still too raw for all concerned.

Emilie and Sigrid's room was no more than three by four metres, a storeroom really, but they were happy to be out of the overcrowded camps, the elements and to have a roof over their heads. All Sigrid remembered later was a room the size of a doll's house, not a flatlette but a *roomlette.*

Another incident vaguely embedded in her memory was when Sigrid had been quite sick. She woke up, bathed in perspiration all alone in the room. *Where is Mutti? Not her gone too?* she wondered feverishly. Sigrid crawled out of bed, crossed the hallway into the freezing stairwell. There she stood on the icy stone floor looking for Mutti. The front door to the building opened, and Mother appeared, 'Oh, Sigrid!' she shrieked.

'It will be a miracle if that child does not die from pneumonia. How could you leave her all alone, sick as she is?' harangued the owner from behind the slightly opened door of her living quarters.

Well, Mother was out looking for work and thought that she might just quickly sneak out, but as is often the case, it took much longer than planned. The queues were too lengthy. From what Sigrid recalled next, Mother had her standing naked in bed, rubbing her body with warm oil. Feeling weak, Sigrid slumped against the wall behind her, leaving a big oily smudge on Frau Lindbaum's storeroom wall. Mother did not know whether to laugh or cry. Of course, Sigrid's health was more important than the landlady's certain verbal reprimand.

A pleasant event in Sigrid's memory of that time was a day in late summer. Sitting behind Mother on a bicycle, they had cycled with a lone unemployed male into the country near Bad Homburg. The young man knew of some apples that had ripened, ready for picking. And pick them they did: Mother and Sigrid came home with a rucksack full, as much as the bicycle allowed. The sweet-sour taste of these apples was to remain with Sigrid, and no fruit that had passed her lips since ever tasted as glorious as those freshly picked apples.

In time, Emilie found a few hours work at a doctor's practice. Sigrid started regular schooling at the Karmeliterschule. A few years later, the two moved to better accommodation in Bornheimer Landstrasse. Here at least, they had two rooms located on the fifth level of a nineteenth-century apartment block. One room was facing the street, while the small kitchen faced the inner courtyard. You walked along the corridor to get to it. Emilie spent evenings and nights teaching herself shorthand by transcribing newspaper articles. She also bought an old typewriter and learned how to type.

Sigrid always remembered one very special New Year's Eve. Her mother had sewn a white dress for her. The material was taffeta, and Mother had hand-stitched hundreds of little shiny *paillettes* onto the bodice that sparkled in the light of the candles. They listened to the radio and danced through the narrow room to the latest hit song, which went something like this, 'You do have to travel / From time to time / And even if it's just for the weekend / To prove to other people / That you know a piece of the globe.'

Sigrid would sing the refrain loudly. Mother made a potato salad with two sausages and mustard. She also heated some *Glühwein*. They danced, ate, drank, laughed, sang, got a little tipsy and considered themselves the two luckiest people in the world.

How adaptable human nature is to be able to recover from the hardship of the past sufficiently and willingly to start afresh again. Here they were, two survivors from a family of originally four, a typical example of humankind's endurance.

After finishing school, Sigrid found work as a junior in the office of a record company. Like her mother, she learned to use the typewriter and typed orders for people who started to buy records for their new record players. Another aspect of Sigrid's work was to run errands either to the bank, the post office, office suppliers or simply to fill lunch orders. In the wake of the horrors of the past, people were more than ready and receptive to the pleasures of various types of music.

Mother held a secretarial position with IG Metall, a large industrial union on Mainkai. Their living conditions also improved. Mother and daughter settled in a spacious first floor two-bedroom apartment in Grosse Seestrasse. Though sparsely furnished, it was comfortable. In the move from the Lindbaums, Heinz's Agfa camera was lost. 'I have my doubts about that,' Mother muttered more than once. Heinz's *David Copperfield* was kept as a revered memento on the top shelf inside her mother's wardrobe. The dedication by Werner Müller on the first page remained a puzzling element. 'Obviously, a friend of Heinz's from the Malchin Youth Camp,' Mother concluded. Sigrid's treasured carved wooden frame with the photograph depicting her seventh birthday celebration with Heinz filled a prominent place on her low-set bookcase.

The German *Wirtschaftswunder* (economic miracle) had arrived, and better times lay ahead.

Werner

'Don't you know? The war's over?'

'*Du Idiot.*'

Heinz's finals words continued to plague Werner.

Deceived and utterly indoctrinated by Hitler's propaganda apparatus, he had been a willing pawn in the cog of Nazi machinery. When Heinz sank down in front of him, it was as if the scales had lifted from Werner's eyes. All the horrors of war were encapsulated in that final fall of the one true friend he ever had.

The images of what happened later blurred like a serrated, surreal black and white painting. The screaming, commotion, questions, the furore, Black Bulls, Germans, cubs, onlooking civilians, but most of all Heinz's eyes, and the flow of blood soaking his chest while his eyes set questioningly on Werner. Heinz's facial expression changed from disbelief to the faintest of smiles on his last sigh. Werner felt as if Heinz saw something magnificent, as if all the grief in the world had been lifted off his chest. From that significant moment, it was as if Werner was in a paralysed trance.

Werner's recall of how he located his Uncle Otto in Hamburg was hazy. Visions of the enquiries and interrogations by Herr Rindermann intermingled with the images of refugees filling country roads, hard to recognise suburbs and destroyed streetscapes.

Werner was determined never to get close to anyone, to keep to himself.

When Otto handed him Heinz's letter, he wished he was the one who had died.

Dear Werner

In case we miss each other in Neustadt I wanted to tell you how much I enjoyed our times together at the Malchin camp. I know the war won't last much longer. Liberation is almost here.

Thank you again for the 'David Copperfield' book. I really enjoy it and can't wait to discuss it with you.

I am looking forward to spending time with you when this shit is over. We have had some differences of opinion but I'm sure by now you can see through the propaganda they fed us all these years.

I'm planning to see you in Hamburg after I've met up with my mother and little sis. Göttingen is not too far from Hamburg. We'll do hikes, and rides, take more snapshots.

I'll enclose the one we took with the timer on the steps of the observatory. It turned out alright.

See you soon.
Your friend Heinz

'If only. If only I hadn't…'

Werner carved a wooden frame for the photograph taken the autumn of 1944, showing the two boys standing on the winding stairs of Remplin. This was his valued possession. He agonised about searching for Heinz's mother. What would he say? *I'm sorry, it's my fault your son died.* At first, it was his intention to take this course of action without delay. It was a hard step to take, and the more time elapsed, the more difficult it became. Werner made excuses to himself. He didn't know where Heinz's mother was—she would scold him, go to court to have him prosecuted, she would, she would…? His emotions vacillated from searching for her immediately, facing whatever consequences, to putting it off till later. He was not afraid of any penalties. It would have been a catharsis. It would have cleansed him, eased his guilt.

Ultimately, having reached his nadir, he did go to the Red Cross, who had begun to track everybody's whereabouts. German officialdom is known for its efficiency, before, during, and after the Third Reich, be it in the Communist East or Capitalist West. Yes, Werner knew that Frau Hermes lived in Frankfurt with her daughter. He even rode his rigged-up bicycle to Frankfurt, a journey taking him seven days. He was shocked at the devastation of the landscape. Even small villages and isolated farmhouses were destroyed. Exhausted but on high alert he waited in front of the Liliencronstrasse entrance.

When he saw the little girl approach, he blurted, 'Are you Siggi?' in such a manner that she got a fright and started to nod vigorously. He panicked when he heard the apartment owner's cacophony from the opened window, 'What do you think you are doing here? Loitering? Move. *Dalli, dalli,* or I'll call the police.'

Werner thrust his letter of confession abruptly into the girl's hands almost shouting, 'Give this to your mother.' Then he turned and peddling furiously, he fled, collapsing on the side of the road before the long trek back to Hamburg.

Despite his intellectual ability Werner now had difficulty adjusting to the last years of high school. At the time of Heinz's killing, no psychological counselling services or debriefing of any kind were available. Victims just had to manage as best as they could or not at all. Otto tried to console. He suggested a walk along the river Elbe. They found a bench close to the water's edge.

'Werner, you won't know this, but during the Weimar Republic of 1918 till 1933, radical groups clashed. In the 1928 bloodbath between the communists and the police, hundreds were injured, some were killed. The 1929 Wall Street Crash prompted the Americans to withdraw all their capital from our German industry, which unsurprisingly collapsed. That led to so much unemployment. People became destitute. Little wonder that the Nazi Party, which promised voters fast solutions, rose to be the second largest party in 1930.'

He paused, got a handkerchief, blew his nose, and continued, 'The government's futile attempt to finance unemployment insurance, while having to pay reparation to the victorious powers of the First World War, did not alleviate the economic depression. Therefore—and I am by no means defending what I am saying next—Hitler and his Nazi Party gained power.'

Otto pulled his cap over the ears. Werner stared at the ripples and reflections on the water. Following his gaze, Otto continued, 'It's getting a bit chilly. We can go to the *Kneipe* (pub) around the corner. In a minute. But it's best I tell you here rather than there. Where was I? Yes, 1933. Since no one seemed to be able to form an effective government, Hitler, in the spirit of political reactionism, led the crisis-ridden republic, and was sworn into office. And with that, the terror started.'

Looking straight into Werner's eyes, Otto's voice wavered, 'You grew up in the euphoria with Hitler's disciples. You were sucked into the megalomania. I was in Norway. Anyway, your father and I didn't see eye to eye on the political front. Nonetheless, I should have made more of an effort to be with you. But I did not want to interfere, and I could not bear the political fervour of your dad.'

Otto took Werner's hands, 'But let me tell you, while you are the product of the political times; the intense brainwashing, growing up immersed in this fanatical environment, yes, what you did, led to a fatal outcome but, and here is the big but, you were only thirteen. You were misled. You had no one to offer a different perspective. Meeting your friend Heinz offered an alternative, albeit, from what you told me, a short one. And, after all, he was also only fourteen. What I am trying to say, Werner, you were involved in an accident. Yes, you were misguided. Misguided by whom? By the *Führer*, first and foremost. By the Hitler machinery, the Hitler Youth organisation. By your battalion leader. By your father, who was blinded by party politics and working for the government. Though you did not see too much of him.'

Clearing his throat and letting go of Werner's hands, 'What I mean to say is, you are young, you can see now what you did, or could not see then. You are remorseful. You've learnt your lesson. Get on with your life. You've got it in front of you. I believe in you, Werner.'

'Thank you, Otto. Uncle Otto,' is all Werner could mutter.

In an endeavour to get his nephew out of depression, Otto recommended that Werner should start an apprenticeship as a carpenter. He had the physical ability, and Otto felt that being useful with his hands might alleviate some of the teen's pain. With so much rebuilding and new construction work around, it would provide the young man with lasting career prospects. He was certainly smart enough to make something out of it, if only he showed an interest.

Werner finished his apprenticeship after three years. For his graduation, Otto presented Werner with a carpenter's *Latthammer*. The handle was engraved with the initials 'WM' and made of ash tree. Yet, Werner did not derive much pleasure, nor found the prospect of working as a carpenter particularly satisfying. Being a reliable worker, he had no problems during the early 1950s finding a job with Hamburg's municipal construction company.

Otto was fully aware of Werner's talent and unfulfilled potential. He tried all sorts of tricks to get his nephew out of the rut into which he had slid. As Werner did not socialise with his fellow workers, nor with anyone else for that matter, Otto took his nephew under his wing. In the summer, Otto invited Werner to come fishing with him at the Binnen Alster, or join him for a beer in St Pauli, where only ten years later the Beatles would commence their path to worldwide mega-stardom.

In the winter, Otto dragged Werner into the inner city's *gemütliche* (cosy) and smoky tea rooms. There they drank hot tea with rum, in which the lumps of dark-brown *Kandis* (raw sugar) slowly dissolved and rose as dark clouds in a golden liquid to the surface. They hunched over their chess board, smoked, sipped on their tea, focussing silently on their game.

Other times Otto took Werner to one of the jazz cellars, where the air was thick with smoke. They sat solemnly listening to Dixie and Swing, tapping their feet to the rhythm of the beat. But no matter what Otto tried, and try he did, the dear old uncle, nothing jolted Werner out of his deep melancholy.

However, Werner did respond to Otto playing classical records on his new gramophone. His uncle observed silently, *He transforms in an almost trancelike manner, his features relax and his worry lines smooth out.* Otto introduced Werner to his collection of Bach concerti. Losing himself in the compositions, Werner sat listening quietly. Coming home after work one evening, Otto had a surprise for Werner.

'Why don't you get away from all this shit here? The gloomy weather, the rain and constant drizzle. Have a fresh start, Werner. Go to Australia, where the sun is. They're looking for young skilled people like you. Look what I've found.'

On behalf of an Australian scheme to recruit tradesmen, German authorities placed ads in the press and on radio. Otto handed Werner an advertisement out of the *Frankfurter Allgemeine* newspaper. It described that commencing in 1949 the Snowy Mountains Hydro-Electric Scheme diverted three rivers in the southeast of Australia to provide irrigation to the eastern part of the continent and generate hydroelectric power. This was to be the most complex, multi-purpose hydro-scheme in the world. It would encompass eighty kilometres of aqueducts, one hundred and forty kilometres of tunnels, sixteen large dams, five above-ground power stations and two underground.

Fourteen major Australian, American and French contractors and consortiums employed one hundred thousand people, many of whom came from a Europe left in ruins and rubble. From the end of World War II till 1954, Australia was asked by the United Nations to accept over one hundred and eighty-two thousand Europeans who were either displaced or refugees.

Werner studied the article and the ad. To have a fresh start somewhere else, where nobody knew him or his tainted past, did appeal to him. Apart from his uncle Otto, who tried so hard to help him, but who just wanted to sit at home and potter around in his vegetable patch on his little plot of dirt, his *Schrebergarten,* Werner had nobody to keep him there.

'Alright, I will send in an application to work on that Snowy Mountains Project. It says here that carpenters can apply.'

'Good, remember, I'll support you with whatever you need.'

Even though Werner was a member of the Carpenter's Guild in Germany, the recruitment team of the Snowy Mountains Authority required him to pass the trades test by making wooden louvres. He had no problems making the grade, saying to Otto, 'It's so easy when you know your trade. Thanks for steering me in this direction, Uncle.'

Werner's application was successful.

In 1954 Otto waved goodbye to Werner Mueller, who, in an effort for a genuine new start, had anglicised his surname. It was an emotional farewell that left both with moistened eyes.

During the surge of migrant worker intake, between 1945 and 1965, more than two million immigrants and displaced people, who were attracted by sunshine and a buoyant future, came to Australia. Provided they stayed for two years and worked in Australian government-arranged jobs, they did not have to repay the financial outlay.

Sigrid

The heavy drops of the first Frankfurt spring shower hit the surface of the timber tabletop and bounced like miniature diamonds through the dappled sunlight. Moving puddles covered the balcony floor. Fragmented sounds of the 1960s hit parade from above penetrated the constant patter of the rain. Emilie was sitting in front of the opened balcony door, she gazed at the argentine clouds above the five-storeyed apartment block opposite. It was Saturday afternoon and Sigrid was getting ready to meet her girlfriend, Sonia.

'Ta-Dah! How do I look?'

Sigrid swept into the living room in a black and white polka dot outfit, its wide black belt fastened with a bold shiny silver buckle highlighting her tiny waist. This was further emphasised by the fluted skirt and the V-necked top with short sleeves.

'You look lovely, my dear. I like your hair short like that,' Emilie answered with pride. 'So where are you two off to today?'

'To the jazz club in Sachsenhausen. I'm meeting Sonia at the station, and then we'll walk across the bridge.'

Sigrid grabbed her raincoat, an umbrella, a small barrel-shaped black handbag, kissed her mother on the left cheek and with, '*Tschüss Mutti,*' headed for the front door.

'Don't you want to wait till the shower is over?'

'If I run fast enough, I'll miss the raindrops.' The door closed before Emilie could raise any further objection, and Sigrid was gone.

Sonia Schulz was already waiting outside the main entrance of Frankfurt Central Station. Her voluptuous silhouette stood out against the drab background of the stone wall behind her. She wore a figure-hugging red short-sleeved pullover and a wide-fluted black skirt with the customary wide silver-buckled black belt. She had black high heels and on her right arm hung a bamboo-handled crocodile-patterned handbag. Her blonde hair was swept up in a French twirl, and above her left breast was a fist-sized white camellia brooch, complemented by smaller matching earrings.

Sonia looked a picture of wealth. This was due to Mehdi, her well-to-do older Persian boyfriend. He arrived in Frankfurt a few years after the war ended, met seventeen-year-old Sonia and was charmed by her innocence and raw beauty. She, in turn, was wooed by his attention and lavish lifestyle. After growing up in wartime

Germany and knowing only lean years, it is not surprising that she fell for him. Mehdi sent Sonia to a college where she learned to be a cosmetician and how to dress stylishly. Since his business interests took him on frequent trips back to Persia and to the south of France, Sonia moved into his apartment in Münzgasse.

Around 1944 Sonia's mother Gerda found a new partner, Ludwig, a Bavarian, while her husband Bruno was fighting on the Western Front. Since Gerda's apartment in Schulstrasse was small and she was unable to offer her daughter an education, she was quite happy with Sonia and Mehdi's arrangement after the war.

Bruno, the father of Gerda's children, ended up the loser in this equation. Already in a depressed state because of the years spent in combat, Bruno could not cope with the disappointment of his homecoming. The thought of being reunited with his family had kept him going through the fighting, shelling, dying, injury, mud, lice, hunger, and the all-consuming pain of it all. But for what? To be confronted in his own home by his wife, who had replaced him with a new man, not only a 'Bavarian' but a Bavarian with 'bad breath.'

This was more than a man as sensitive as he could endure. Within days, Bruno ended his life by hanging himself—another post-war casualty. Gerda's older son Wolfgang discovered the body and left not long after for South Africa, where young men were being recruited to work at the mine sites.

Here now stood his beautiful daughter Sonia. Bruno would have been proud to see her. Would he have been happy with her and Mehdi's arrangement? How different life would and could have been if it hadn't been for that wretched war.

'Hi, Sigrid, I am so glad that the rain has stopped. I've been waiting for a while. Got to go to Mother's, promised to drop off this record. It's Ludwig's birthday, he likes this oompah music, and she hassled me till I agreed to take it over. It won't take too long. We'll just do a little divert around the railway yard and then take the tram into Sachsenhausen. Do you mind?'

'No, I don't,' Sigrid answered hesitantly. The two girls first met while roller skating at Mainkai. Each aspired to follow star skater Marika Kilius's stardom. They literally bumped into each other on the rink, started a conversation and became friends. Their age difference did not matter. Both young women liked to skate, go to movies, ice cafés and venues which played jazz and where they could dance. Other common interests were fashion, makeup and being blissfully young and optimistic.

'Good then, let's go.' Both walked in their high heels, trying not to get caught in the cobble stones, their skirts swinging from side to side. They chatted about everything and nothing and reached Schulstrasse in no time at all.

'Hi, Ma, I'm here. Oh, what's up. Wolfi? I don't believe it. When did you get here? How long have you been here? Nobody tells me anything.'

Slightly sulky, Gerda replied, 'Couldn't tell you, cos I didn't know myself. He only arrived last night.'

Wolfgang beamed broadly, 'Hey, sis. My oh my, you do scrub up nicely. Don't you look great?' He embraced Sonia warmly and kissed her on each cheek. Turning to Sigrid, he said, 'Good afternoon, lovely lady.'

'This is my friend, Sigrid. We're on our way to the jazz club in Sachsenhausen,' Sonia enthused.

'So, you two are off to town, eh? A jazz club? I wouldn't mind a bit of jazz, better than that Bavarian oompah and Mother will be happy to have the evening alone with *Kőnig* Ludwig.' He raised the tone of his voice slightly, 'Do you mind if I join you?'

'Well, what do you think, Sigrid? I don't mind. I haven't seen Wolfi for a few years. What do you think?'

'It's um, ok with me.'

Without too much fuss, the three young people left Schulstrasse and headed to Sachsenhausen. This arrangement of going out under the unexpected protection of her brother Wolfgang suited Sonia. Mehdi did not like Sonia to venture too far without his supervision. At times Sonia felt like she was being kept in a gilded cage.

Since Mehdi was well-known in Persian circles and appeared to have contacts everywhere, it seemed to Sonia that she was watched, or even followed on occasions. However, the alternative was to live with no prospects on a couch at her mother's flat. At least Mehdi provided her with an introduction to a life beyond her expectations and gave her a feeling of self-worth. Deep down, she hoped that one day he would marry her. And he did—eventually.

Before they even arrived at the jazz club, they could hear the beat of the music.

Frankfurter Jazz Band

People were popping out of the front entrance, which led into a crowded and smoky brick-walled cellar. Close to the wall on the right, the bar was lit up by candles in wax-covered wine bottles. A couple of ancient beer barrels stood next to the counter under dimly lit globes covered by tin pots. People were huddled around holding their beer glasses. On an elevated stage, the band stood, or rather swung. They consisted of double bass, guitars, trumpet, clarinet, and a banjo player. True to their name, the *Frankfurter Hot Lips Dixie* were bopping away with their lead singing *When The Saints Go Marching In.*

The three squeezed their way through the crowd. Couples were swaying, bumping and moving to the beat. Somehow, they managed to find a space where Wolfgang took hold of Sigrid's waist and led her into the movement of the general swing of those on the dance floor. Sigrid felt a warm sensation in her stomach as Wolfgang pressed her close to him. Every now and again, she caught a whiff of his masculine scent. She liked the strong feel of his muscled arms and his wide broad grin as he swung her around whenever there was an opening in the crowd.

After they had quite a workout on the dance floor, dripping in perspiration, Wolfgang led Sigrid outside, indicating that he was going to get them a drink and look for Sonia. Sigrid was not sure about her feelings. While she'd had a few boyfriends, she never went any further than kissing. The greatest shame would be to fall pregnant without being married; that was well and truly drummed into her. There was gossip about girls who got into 'trouble' and ruined their lives. Sigrid did not want to be one of them. Years later, a mature Sigrid would reflect how society's mores had changed. She now lived in an era when social media and schoolteachers taught girls like Isabella about contraception from a young age.

Wolfgang was unlike the boys Sigrid had been out with. He had a streak of adventure and was very manly. He reminded her of her brother Heinz, the way he took control. She had forgotten how much she missed Heinz.

Wolfgang

Wolfgang Schulz did not escape the psychological impact of the Third Reich. Like Heinz and Werner, young Wolfgang was fleetingly sent to various *KLV*, government-regulated dispatches of children to the country. Subsequently, he also ended up in the Hitler Youth camps.

At the end of the war, motivated by a desire to escape the overall chaos, Wolfgang was traumatised after finding his father hanging from the rafter. His mother's living arrangement with Ludwig rubbed salt into his wounded heart. When the opportunity arose to work in the mines in South Africa, Wolfgang did not hesitate to inform his sister Sonia, 'I've found a job near Johannesburg, I'm leaving.'

After working in South Africa for some months, Wolfgang met Gerald Gaythorne at a café. An art teacher in his early fifties, Gerald was attracted to blonde and blue-eyed Wolfgang. He started a conversation enquiring about Germany and whether he liked working in the mines. Flattered by so much attention, Wolfgang agreed to regular meetings with Gerald. Then, one day, out of the blue, Gerald extended his right arm over his balding scalp, stroked his sparse hairline with his hand, and proposed with insouciance, 'My friend Nick runs a painting and decorating business. You can work for him, Wolfgang. It will be much better for you. You won't come home with coal dust all over you.' As if reading Wolfgang's mind, he added, 'You can break your contract with the mines. I'll help you.'

Gerald arranged for Wolfgang to live in his apartment as his companion. Under Nick's wing, Wolfgang learned the tricks of the trade.

Gerald introduced Wolfgang to a world hitherto unknown to the young protégé. As a keen collector of artworks, his benefactor imparted to Wolfgang an understanding of the finer nuances of paintings. Gerald was also a great conversationalist; they were wined and dined, and frequently invited by the arty set of Johannesburg society. They toured around Cape Town, Durban and came close to the wild animals in Kruger National Park.

Gerald took Wolfgang to Italy some years later, the focus being the great art works at the *Uffizi* in Florence. It was there that Gerald booked himself into a four-week art workshop under the tutelage of Florentine painter Annigoni.

Overcome by homesickness at the thought of being in the proximity of Germany, Wolfgang suggested, he could catch a train to Frankfurt to see his mother and sister.

'Yes, by all means. You go.' Stroking his forehead in familiar manner, Gerald added, 'Hmm, that would fit perfectly well with my plans.'

The agreement was, Wolfgang should spend four weeks in Germany and then join Gerald in Rome before flying back to Johannesburg together.

After Sonia introduced Wolfgang to Sigrid, he surprised himself by taking the plunge and asking cheekily if he could go with them to the jazz club in Sachsenhausen. At that stage, Wolfgang was gripped by a desire not to return to his living arrangement with Gerald.

He liked Sigrid. She was cute and fresh, not like the artificially sophisticated women that formed part of Gerald's circle of friends. He was captivated by her impish mien, and the slight gap between her front teeth, which her cropped hair accentuated. He felt he must act quickly to gain her favour. *This girl is very charming; she has no problems getting boyfriends. Gerald will want me to return to Johannesburg. If, on the one hand, I'm involved with her, then, on the other, I'll be free of my arrangement with him.*

While all this played on his mind, Sigrid was unaware of his emotional upheaval.

Sigrid and Wolfgang had a relatively short courtship. In a fit of braggadocio, he slipped an engagement ring on her finger, and they were married within four weeks. Wolfgang did not return to Gerald and South Africa. For a period— intended to be brief—*I couldn't bear to live in a cramped space like my mother,* the newlyweds did move into the bigger apartment of Sigrid's mother Emilie in Grosse Seestrasse. Wolfgang found work as a house painter and Sigrid continued with her job at the record company.

It was not long before Sigrid noticed traits in Wolfgang's personality that perturbed the early period of their marriage. She bought a bunch of tulips for her mother's birthday and put them on the kitchen bench. While she manoeuvered a cake onto a plate, Wolfgang waltzed in, swiped the bunch of flowers with a flourishing, 'I've got a surprise for your birthday, Emilie,' and presented the flowers to her as if he had arranged it.

Over time tension started to develop in the household. Emilie tried to remain neutral, but occasionally she could not help herself, 'Some people would have more initiative to do something constructive, Wolfgang.'

Sigrid tried to defend her husband and was caught in the middle.

Several years later, to everyone's surprise, Wolfgang found an advertisement by the Australian Government in the *Frankfurter Allgemeine* inviting tradespeople and couples to work in Australia. It was a similar scheme to the one Werner had applied to in the 1950s.

After the initial euphoria of returning to Germany, Wolfgang found it difficult to settle down. Having savoured the open space and blue sky of South Africa, he wanted to escape the cold climate and the long German winters. With a sense of adventure, he saw a move to Australia as a panacea. *Get away from suffocating and bureaucratic old Europe and start a new adventure in Australia. It won't cost us anything if we stay for two years. That'll go quickly. No risk here. We get a holiday for free. With Siggi, it would have to be better than my previous set-*

up in South Africa. And—I won't have to put up with the mother-in-law's smart remarks anymore.

Oblivious to Wolfgang's main motivation, Sigrid also saw this as a means for them to build a better future. *Living with Mother is so problematic. We just don't seem to be able to get an apartment of our own. I'm so sick of the constant bickering. I wish Wolfi was steadier. Surely, he'll feel better with a fresh start. Plus, sunshine every day. Great. Yes, why not try our luck in Australia!*

6. Werner - Australia 1954–2013

Werner's arrival

In 1954 *MS Skaubryn*, a ship chartered by the Snowy Mountains Authority to transport German tradesmen to Australia, departed Bremerhaven with Werner and more than one thousand two hundred migrants, skilled workers and labourers. For over five weeks, they journeyed via Port Said through the Suez Canal to Melbourne, the same route Sigrid and Wolfgang were to take more than a decade later. Werner shared a cabin with four other Germans and struck up a friendship with Hans, a teenager who, like himself, had no family. Hans confided to Werner, 'I can't see a future in all this chaos at home. I want to put the past behind me and have a fresh start somewhere. I don't care if that means snow or sun. If sun, then all the better. I am longing for a new life.'

Together they did not participate in the strike for improved conditions on board the ship, led by baker Johann, 'We can't have the same slop as these people who are displaced,' Johann reasoned vociferously. 'They are getting a free trip. Didn't we get a contract to work in Australia straight away?'

The strike only lasted two days.

Crossing the equator, Johann threw his heavy coat overboard. 'I won't ever need that one again. I'm sailing to the land of the sun.'

Some tentatively followed his lead, but Werner thought about the definition of *snowy mountains* and reasoned that it might be best to hang onto his winter coat, a choice he was not to regret.

In Melbourne, after promising to stay in touch, Werner parted company with Hans, who travelled by a wooden train to the assembly camp of Bonegilla.

After passing yet another carpentry test, this time set by the Building Workers Industrial Union, Werner was bussed with other skilled recruits to East Camp in Cooma.

Werner was astonished by the vastness of a barren-beige scenery with taupe to mustard-coloured vegetation spanned by an intense blue sky. It was devoid of snow or high peaked rocky mountains, like in Austria. Bewitched by the foreign landscape, his frame of mind changed to confusion when the bus stopped at the railway station. He could not comprehend the sign: *Beware of poisonous snakes, spiders, and venereal disease!*

The sight of German carpenters moving around in their traditional black wide-bottomed corduroy trousers, with mother-of-pearl buttoned waistcoats, and homburg hats, only added to his confusion. *I hoped I'd left all that behind me. Have I entered a time warp on another planet?*

Werner's uncomplaining attitude was further tested on his first night. The early Australian spring weather produced below-freezing temperatures against which the thin walls of the hut, to which he had been allocated, did not provide much protection. He was thankful for not having to sleep in one of the tents for workers and to have kept his coat by not following Johann's example at the equator crossing. The primitive conditions of his accommodation and the camp atmosphere in general did not upset him but tied in with his disposition and motto, 'The harsher, the better.'

After a fitful sleep on a wire bed base without a mattress, Werner's mood lifted at the sight of a magnificent, sunny blue sky. *Perhaps this was not such a bad move after all?*

Werner was put to work immediately building new barracks, office buildings and workshops. To meet the demand of the growing settlement, houses were prefabricated in Cooma and then shifted around on a truck, a concept hitherto unknown and initially intriguing to Werner, who was used to working on immovable sites. He conceded that these dwellings were solidly built and insulated to endure the journey and climate. Open-mouthed and perplexed, he watched as a truck with the signage 'Danger – Wide Load Following,' rolled along the bumpy roads.

'You obviously haven't seen one of those before, mate. Them motor lorries have only replaced the horse and cart recently. You should've been here at the beginning of the year when horses and sulkies delivered groceries. This ain't like the big city, you know. You're in the country here, mate.'

'Ist zsat so?' Werner, not understanding most of what was said, replied to the short, stocky workman. He wondered what groceries had to do with houses on trucks and horses.

Having passed several skill tests back home, and since arriving Down Under, his confidence was tested by his inability to work the hard Australian timber despite the aid of his trusty *Latthammer*. If the wood was aged more than two years, it was extremely difficult to yield. Werner soon copied the Australian style as explained by his fellow carpenter. 'What you do, mate, you drill a hole into the hardwood. Put grease into the hole and on the nail and then, only then, you hammer it in. Like so.'

'They didn't teach me that during my carpentry apprenticeship,' Werner gasped.

Werner's loner temperament was suited to the rigid routine of getting up early for a 6:30 am breakfast. He worked hard until lunch at 12 and continued in the same vein until dinner at 5:30 pm. He did not enjoy the mush presented as food and missed his *Rollmops*, sour gherkins, and potato salad. But overall, he thrived in the rigorous conditions of camp life.

Most of the recruits were single. Day and night, they could be seated boisterously along the tables of the mess halls. Earning good money coupled with boredom added to the workers' attraction of partaking in drinking bouts and playing card games. While these serious money transactions took place, Werner kept to himself, and his money remained in his pockets. He returned to the single men's quarters to read or sleep. When alone, using his newly purchased turntable, he indulged listening ad nauseam to the record of Wilhelm Kempff playing Bach's Prélude in C Major. This recording was Otto's departure present.

Werner's initial worries about possible hostilities by other nationalities towards him as a German turned out to be unwarranted. Outnumbered by the newcomers, Cooma locals seemed to be hesitant towards them, sometimes bordering on suspicion. Unsurprisingly, they were consistent with their: we-speak-English-here attitude. Werner took the occasional *squarehead, Kraut* and *Hun* in his stride and quickly realised that the literal meaning of the word *bastard* was used in an affectionate sense.

His expectation of Australia being a classless society was tainted by the realisation that social hierarchy did exist: waged labourers ranked second to administrative staff. But he soon developed a sense of pride to be part of the Snowy Mountains Hydro-Electric Scheme, the world's most complex, multi-reservoir system to provide power and irrigation on a massive scale.

Werner's first winter further justified the purpose of his thick coat. A blizzard engulfed Cooma and the snow was so heavy that skiers were trapped ninety kilometres north-west. Not being a skier himself, he was more interested investing his spare hours in learning the English language. Werner conscientiously attended compulsory classes and responded extremely well to the instructions of Mrs Bishop. She was the wife of the Anglican minister and followed the Commonwealth Migrant English Teaching curriculum.

He never forgot her prophetic words, 'Werner, if you keep applying yourself with such enthusiasm, you will do well in this country. You will be able to achieve great things. Indeed, whatever you set your heart on will land in your lap.'

A burden lifted off his chest. Someone, unaware of his past, was here instilling hope, optimism, and a glimmer of purpose into his life. *Perhaps, in this country, I can do something worthwhile after all?* Uncle Otto had tried to do the same for him back home. However, the insistent presence of Werner's brooding memories, Hamburg's devastated surroundings and prevailing austere atmosphere made a new start exceedingly difficult for him.

Werner now applied himself. He saved his money. While some workers drank, Werner enjoyed running and sometimes playing in the German football team at camp. He did not get involved in the occasional squabble between the German and Polish players.

After fulfilling his two-year contract, Werner decided to remain, continue to save money and buy a second-hand two-door green Morris Minor. He liked to explore the surrounding area in his car, roads permitting, and appreciated the vastness of the hazy hued landscape on a hot day. Boulders, embedded like rough marbles in the soil, surrounded by dark beige-coloured sparse vegetation, was a sight so unlike the lush forests at home. The all-encompassing soft purple mist on the horizon below the pale blue sky—apparently, this desolate scenery seemed what his soul yearned for.

By attending further evening studies, Werner vastly improved his English language skills. He kept a schedule that occupied every spare minute, particularly when Mr Prosser took an interest and taught him first aid. This enabled Werner to eventually become a volunteer with St John Ambulance, where the ethos of being a Good Samaritan and helping without a thought of reward appealed to him. Instead of playing in football matches, he now proudly attended as first aid officer. *I am doing something useful, and I feel good being able to ease the pain of injured players. Healing others might help me to heal myself.*

A new start

As a keen athlete, Werner followed German long-distance runner Herbert Schade. Though he was careful never to mention his adolescent involvement with the *HJ*, having quickly understood the Australian feelings and prejudice attached to anything associated with Germany, and Hitler in particular. During the 1952 Helsinki Summer Olympics, Schade won the five-thousand-metre bronze medal. On the day of that race, Uncle Otto had taken Werner to the pub on the corner to listen to the radio broadcast. To Werner's immense joy, Schade was now competing in Australia in the five-thousand and ten-thousand-metre events at the 1956 Summer Olympics in Melbourne.

The day before the ten-thousand-metre race, Werner and four other workers travelled in his overcrowded Morris to Melbourne. On Friday, the twenty-third of November, they arrived at the stadium.

Werner's friend Harald was very excited, 'I can't wait for the twenty-five participants to compete in the ten-thousand-metre race. They are coming from fifteen nations.'

'Schade is bound to do well,' Werner answered optimistically.

Werner and other Germans were cheering Schade. The Polish group came to cheer their favourite Zdzislaw Krzyszkowiak. However, both cheer squads were disappointed as the Soviet Vladimir Kuts came first, Krzyszkowiak fourth and Schade ninth.

'*So schade* (such a pity), always those Russians, eh?' Harald lamented wittily.

Both the German and Polish spectators behaved with civility towards each other, putting any political differences aside.

Returning to Cooma, Werner's original impression flooded back to him, that of a desolate country. He felt unsettled after his exposure to the hustle and bustle of Melbourne and the restaurants on Lygon Street. Though in comparison to the small surrounding communities of Adaminaby, Berridale and Jindabyne, Cooma, despite its many rickety wooden dwellings, was now a town with nightclubs and a hospital. But it did lack the enticement of a large city.

During the late 1950s, the Snowy Mountains Scheme relocated townships to make way for new dams. Werner continued to work on projects like moving the two-storey bank building eight kilometres to the site of the new Adaminaby. The task of moving houses no longer fazed him. He also took part in downing his tools for the four minutes of the Melbourne Cup Day standstill. Participating rather than being an onlooker, Werner strengthened his

House on wheels

commitment to a new life by taking out Australian citizenship in 1958. Swearing the oath to the English Queen did feel strange, but it was part of the ritual, had to be done, and the whole ceremony proved to be quite moving for him.

He came out of his shell and went to see movies like 'High Society' starring Bing Crosby and the beautiful Grace Kelly. Werner responded positively to Harald's enticement, 'Let's go to the new Pasha nightclub. They've got combos from Yugoslavia, Greece, Italy, and Hungary. It's supposed to be quite sophisticated.'

'Why not, let's go tonight.'

'We might even have a dance with the nurses from the local hospital.'

The two friends went, had a couple of drinks, but due to the raucous behaviour of the nurses, lost the courage to ask.

A yearning stirred in Werner to put some structure into his life. He gained huge enjoyment and satisfaction volunteering with St John Ambulance at the local football matches on weekends. He had endeavoured to assimilate in Cooma, but since his trip to the Olympic Games missed what reminded him of home. The lure of what represented a 'cosmopolitan' eatery, an Italian restaurant opening its doors to Cooma residents, did not change his mind. Werner was ready to leave what had been his home for the last six years.

He did not renew his contract in 1960 and packed his few belongings into his Morris, farewelled Harald and others, and drove to Melbourne. There he took lodgings in Carlton and had no problems starting work as a carpenter. He was employed in various jobs, one of which were the renovations at the university. During lunch breaks, he sat under a tree, ate his sandwiches, and watched the young students meander across the lawn, crouched in groups, debating issues, or sitting by themselves reading or writing. Werner liked this environment of learnedness. It appealed to his intellect. He began to reflect on his lost years of education and regretted not having finished his studies in Hamburg when Uncle Otto urged him to do so. The seed planted by Uncle Otto and Mrs Bishop to further educate himself, now grew into a solid desire to complete his education.

Werner enrolled in night classes to work towards his matriculation. During the day, he worked at his trade and at night, he attended classes and spent the rest of his time studying and completing assignments. Three years later, he proudly received his matriculation certificate showing straight A's.

Finding a vocation

Born out of a need to cleanse himself of his deep-rooted mea culpa, exacerbated by the incident of helplessly watching Heinz's last moments, Werner wanted to do some good for his fellow human beings. He felt the crowning of achievements in his life would be to become a medical doctor. *I am ambitious, not afraid of hard work. I like studying. I've got good references. I volunteered successfully with St John Ambulance. If I set myself a target and do some serious planning, I should be able to achieve my goal.* Werner had also read that the Australian Government encouraged mature-age applicants to enter universities. He applied to study Medicine.

He was accepted, providing he passed all his subjects with satisfactory grades, and committed himself to work in the country after his graduation and registrar internship. Otto was very pleased when he received this news, '*er macht was aus sich*, he makes something of himself. *I always knew he would.*'

For over six years Werner assiduously studied for his MBBS. In one of the university's nearby suburbs, he shared rental accommodation with four other students and worked as a casual carpenter. Other than attending the occasional athletic event, Werner permitted himself little time for pleasure. Though when the Oscar Peterson Trio performed at the town hall, he bought a ticket. The smooth symphonic sounds of jazz transported him back to the jazz cellars into which Uncle Otto had once dragged him. He formed a plan to bring his uncle out for his graduation.

Occasionally Werner went with fellow students to the local pub or parties, but he never got close to any of the girls who were always around. Girls were attracted to his Germanic handsomeness: his square-jawed face, his straight nose, his piercing grey eyes. Furthermore, having an air of aloofness added to his allure. Had he wanted, he could have had a string of girlfriends, but other than dating sporadically, Werner buried himself in his studies.

As the day of his graduation drew nearer, he somehow hoped Uncle Otto would have been able to share in the experience of obtaining his admission into the medical profession. But Uncle Otto could not make it, he was too frail for such a strenuous journey. Not shying away from celebrating his achievement, Werner attended his graduation ceremony and walked onto the stage of the university auditorium. Receiving his Bachelor of Medicine and Bachelor of Surgery from the Chancellor filled him with pride. It was one of those moments when he had wished that his mother, father and sister Anna or his Uncle Otto were present. He was also thinking of his friend Heinz, who, he felt, would have given his nod of approval. The award for his success on this ceremonial occasion gave him the confidence to think that he would prove his worth to them all.

Uncle Otto passed away soon after Werner's graduation. His last thoughts belonged to his ward, that he would be alright and that he turned his involvement in Heinz's death into something positive. Werner's successful medical studies were proof of that.

Having lost his last relative, mentor and friend, Werner threw himself into his work with renewed vigour as an intern at a major hospital. Putting in long hours with little sleep did not leave much time for troubling thoughts or other activities. His supervising professors and the other interns regarded him well. Werner excelled in his work and study, which involved research and reports. Though in tandem with his busy schedule, he partook in the occasional long-distance race at the athletics track.

One night, he visited the town hall to hear the Jacques Loussier Trio. Werner enjoyed the Trio's jazzed-up version of Bach, proving his love of classical music could be in harmony with converted interpretational jazz. Werner's free time became more limited after commencing work as a Resident Medical Officer, especially with the extra training in surgery. He thought about working in private practice once he completed his Senior Residency. A position became available at the regional hospital in Wodonga, where he commenced in 1971 as Junior Registrar. This furthered his particular interest in wound healing. He remained as a Senior Registrar for another year.

Not yet forty years of age, Werner gained a probationary position in a local medical practice in Wodonga. He saw no need to look elsewhere for employment, the work experience in Wodonga had been good. He was ready to reciprocate. The bright lights and life of the big cities held not too much interest for him and the distance to occasional concert performances in Melbourne was no hurdle for his trusty Morris, though he was now ready for a new VW.

Dr Rufus McIvery ran the Pearce Street Medical Practice. He was in his early sixties. His ethos of focusing on individual, patient-centred care in line with the professional standards set by the Royal Australian College of General Practitioners echoed Werner's sentiments. Dr McIvery introduced Werner to the staff, 'You'll be working with Roy Cooke. This is also his first appointment,' he paused and continued, 'after his residency. Eva Webster is our nurse. And you have already met our receptionist, Diane Miller. She manages our new paper-based record system.'

Werner fitted in well with the team. All had a good work ethic and respect for each other and the patients. While the unpredictability of emergencies presented challenges, Werner's analytical mind and compassion enabled him to accurately diagnose medical conditions which he treated with dedication and general concern for the welfare of his patients. A few of his female patients fell in love with him, but he dealt with their advances in a reserved and professional manner. After a few months, Werner passed his probationary contract with flying colours. The time passed, and before Christmas, he had worked at the practice for nearly a year.

Werner and Eva

As part of the medical practice's annual tradition, Diane organised a Christmas get together at the local restaurant. As much as Werner disliked these kinds of events, he could not really offend his co-workers by not attending, and he had to admit to himself he did like their company.

The evening started with a few pre-dinner drinks, followed by a set menu arranged by Diane. Werner commented on the differences in Christmas traditions. 'If you were in Germany, you would be eating goose instead of roast chicken with gravy and baked vegetables. Of course, there it would be cold and snowing.'

'Yes, that's right. I remember when I was in England a few years' ago,' Eva concurred, 'it was freezing.'

Liqueurs followed the Christmas pudding, and as a special treat, Diane managed to get a bottle of *Jägermeister*. Like all good office receptionists and assistants, she had done her detective work and discovered Werner's partiality to that drink. 'Well, my favourite botanical elixir. That is a surprise. Thank you.' All sampled the drink with varying reactions. The party ended when the wife of Rufus arrived to drive him home. Diane was collected by her husband. They gave Roy a lift home, and their offer to drop Eva off was interrupted by Werner's, 'I'll give you a lift home, Eva, if you like.'

'Oh, thank you. Are you sure it's not out of your way?'

'Not at all. It will be my pleasure.' Werner surprised himself by his unaccustomed spontaneity. He always found Eva Webster to be pleasant. Her reserved nature and professionalism, the calm way she dealt with emergencies, and her attractive looks made her a pleasure to be around. She had green eyes, symmetrical features, wore her ash-blonde hair in a bob and was slimly built with a well-proportioned body.

Emboldened by a few shots of *Jägermeister,* and eager to show off his new VW, Werner impulsively took Eva's arm, escorted her to his car, opened the door for her, then settling into his seat asked, 'Which direction are we taking, Eva?' This auspicious question was to determine the rest of their relationship.

Stopping outside Eva's townhouse, Werner pulled her towards him and what was intended to be a kiss of affection turned into one of passion as their tongues touched. Both were seized by intense physical longing. Eva's clichéd, 'Would you like to come in for a cup of coffee?' was the necessary trigger for both to hastily exit the car and for Werner to closely follow Eva into the entrance of her townhouse.

Eva overcame a moment of awkwardness by cheerily asking if Werner would like a coffee or another glass of *Jägermeister*, which she miraculously produced. Werner was indeed very surprised. 'Obviously, my likes and tastes have been discussed at work.'

'Well, just a tad,' Eva admitted ruefully.

They settled onto the couch and sipped on their chilled glasses of the brown liquid. After some silent moments, Eva asked, 'What are you thinking?'

'Oh, I just thought it might be nice to lie down for a while.'

'Really? That's amazing. I thought exactly the same. Well, why don't we? The bed in my bedroom is more comfortable than this couch.'

As if by command, they both got up instantly, and Werner followed Eva up the stairs into the bedroom. As they reclined on the double bed, the closeness of their bodies released electricity that connected them like magnets. They were both hungry for love, physically and emotionally, and the primeval nature of the species took its natural, ecstatic and climactic course.

From that moment onwards, Werner and Eva became an item. They were compatible in nature and age.

After completing her nursing qualifications, Eva went to England like so many other ex-patriots of her age at that time. She worked in Cambridge and London hospitals. During the early 1960s, she dated Gerry, an American who was stationed at an army base near Cambridge. They drove in his Triumph Stag sports car through the countryside and up to Ipswich near the sea. During a cocktail party at one of Gerry's mates, Eva had more than her fair share of whiskey. She normally did not drink this, but it was flowing freely and plentifully, and it was just pleasant. Eva's recollection of what happened later was to remain nebulous to her. Apparently, Gerry intended to drive them to a friend's place for the night but had an accident on the way and the car overturned on a bend in the road. Fortunately, neither she nor Gerry was injured.

When Eva woke up, she was lying in a darkened room in a strange place, which turned out to be Gerry's friend's house. From that moment, she never touched whiskey again, and soon after, she stopped dating Gerry. She had a string of other boyfriends, but her independent streak precluded her from allowing herself to become permanently attached to anyone. She just hadn't found the right one.

When she returned to Australia in the late sixties, she found the Australian males she met to be somewhat rough and lacking etiquette. She missed the suave refinement and care some of her gentlemanly suitors had shown back in England. Indeed, she thought with fondness and a slight sense of regret about her earlier admirers. That did not, however, include Gerry.

Eva was quite resigned to spend the rest of her life as a single woman. She had just successfully negotiated a bank loan to purchase her own two-bedroom townhouse in Central Wodonga with views over Les Stone Park. It was still difficult for single women in those days to obtain a real estate loan, and Eva was very proud to have a mortgage over her own four walls.

Not given to emotional outbursts by nature, Eva nonetheless possessed pent up sexuality, and she now felt in perfect physical and spiritual harmony with Werner. She always found him to be handsome and his calm nature appealed to her own reserve. They shared the same empathy for their patients and applied themselves with utter professionalism. Little wonder they agreed to spend their lives together. Eva's sense of humour could accommodate and got used to the occasional relapse into German when Werner, wanting to drive into the countryside, insisted, 'I need a *Tapetenwechsel*' (a change of scenery). They formalised their union and married in the mid-1970s. Werner was forty-two years old. Working together at Pearce Street Medical Centre, as it was called by now, was an asset rather than a hindrance.

The Muellers bought a house on a quarter of an acre at the southern end of Beechworth Road in Wodonga. The house was a Besser block bungalow with lots of glass and a sense of openness which appealed to both. The surrounding grounds consisted of a variety of smallish trees and bushes.

Eva wanted to establish a rural environment, but Werner was not so keen on her idea of keeping chickens. He was inclined to retreat into his study, where he busied himself reading medical journals, and the German classics, which was a habit he started soon after moving into their new home. He was happy surrounded by his collection of books and four framed Leonardo da Vinci prints hanging between the book-lined shelves. These drawings consisted of a foetus in the womb, studies of a shoulder and neck, of arms and hands, and the head of Leda, whose perfect features and peaceful facial expression reminded Werner of his little sister Anna. He often sat at his desk, deep in thought, his gaze wandering over these drawings in admiration of da Vinci's genius.

Werner stored his extensive collection of Bach records and cassettes on the bottom shelf and often listened to the cantatas. On the middle shelf at eye level was his prized wooden-framed photograph of Heinz and himself on the winding stairs of the observatory in Remplin. Werner told Eva the story of his friendship with Heinz, his briefly misguided youthful ideologies and attempt at redemption. Many a night she roused him out of his nightmares.

'I see Heinz's eyes. He is lying on his side, trying to tell me something. But he can't speak. I'm buried up to my neck in the trench. I can't move. *Die Panzer fahren über mich.* They are rolling closer, closer. They are so near. They are going to roll over us now. The noise of the thundering engines and gun fire drowns everything. And I can't move.'

Wiping the perspiration off Werner's forehead, Eva tried to comfort him.

'Werner, you are safe. You are in Australia. Your nightmare of the past is over. The war is over. Fighting is over. Try to be positive. Think of your numerous patients, how you help them and the good you do. I love you. You are a fine man and a wonderful husband.'

Werner gradually calmed down.

In 1980, Rufus was ready to retire. He gave the Muellers the first option to take over the medical centre. Werner and Eva, after working out their finances, did not hesitate. They accepted his offer and soon became the owners of their medical practice. It was the culmination of their professional aspirations.

Pearce Street Medical Centre was run successfully and efficiently by Werner and Eva Mueller until 2000, when both retired. Due to Werner's increasing problems with arthritis, they decided to move to a warmer climate. They chose Queensland and settled at the Gap in Brisbane.

7. Sigrid - Australia 1966–2013

Sigrid and Wolfgang

During the European autumn of September 1966, migrants Wolfgang, Sigrid, other young people and paying passengers left Bremerhaven aboard the *Angelina Laura* bound for Sydney. A journey that would take six weeks. In a fashion like cattle transportation, four men were allocated per small cabin and four women to another. The ship went via the Suez Canal, before the canal's eight-year closure at the beginning of the Six-Day War. In Port Said, Sigrid and Wolfgang joined a group for a stroll around the harbour. Dark, deeply embedded memories of soldiers infiltrated Sigrid's consciousness. She felt uncomfortable, 'I find all these uniformed men here intimidating, especially with their threatening rifles.'

Nonetheless, after some haggling, they ended up buying a red leather pouffe cover. Those were the days when being oblivious about customs declarations did not result in a hefty fine on entering Australian shores.

The ship's first stop in Australia was Fremantle. It was Sunday, and the area surrounding the harbour and Peter Hughes Drive was deserted.

Sigrid observed, 'There is no person, dog, anybody or anything. Have we landed on the movie set of "On the Beach?" Wasn't that made in Australia? It's so, so post-apocalyptic.' Wolfgang could not offer an explanation.

Days later they arrived in Melbourne from where they were transported by train in wooden railway carriages to the Victorian town of Bonegilla, which was the collection camp for all new arrivals. From there, people were allocated to various regions in Australia. Wolfgang and Sigrid decided to try their luck in Brisbane, a decision based on a chance meeting with a fellow German traveller, Dieter, on the *Angelina Laura*. He was married to an Australian woman from Monto in Queensland, 'This state has a great future. It has plenty of mining resources and construction work. It also has the best climate of all Australian states. That would be the place to go.'

Wolfgang looked at Sigrid, 'Why not try it there?'

'Yes, Brisbane is the capital, isn't it?'

'Sure is,' Dieter confirmed.

Sigrid queried, 'Perhaps we should go there first and see what it's like. We are more used to life in the city.'

Wolfgang nodded, 'You've got a point there.'

'As long as they have jazz clubs,' Sigrid chuckled.

'I don't know about that. It's not really my scene,' was Dieter's contribution, leaving Sigrid pondering about a period in her past that had seemed carefree, oh, so long ago.

The Queensland Government was quite selective as to who should be allowed to settle in their state. The prerequisites included: having learned the English language and having a trade or profession that the government deemed worthy. The Schulz couple met these criteria and were allowed to go to Brisbane. First though, they had to partake in the compulsory bus tour of Albury/Wodonga, which was recommended as a place for newcomers to settle and which seemed in need of populating. Disregarding the enticements, *Make your future and fortune in prosperous Albury/Wodonga,* Wolfgang and Sigrid boarded another wooden train en route to Queensland.

It was a long journey on a slow train, stopping for refreshments at various townships along the way. Sigrid and Wolfgang hopped out of the carriage and collected warm sandwiches made from unfamiliar soggy white bread wrapped in grease-proof paper. As confirmed coffee drinkers, the Schulzes accepted the predictable cup of milky, weak and lukewarm tea with some reluctance. From the carriage window, they saw a landscape enormously different to what they were accustomed to in Germany: parched open plains, undulating hills in faded sandy-brown colours dotted with gum trees, instead of the verdant, modulated greens of the Taunus Forest near Frankfurt. Here kangaroos were hopping beside the track instead of squirrels racing up trees and elegant deer trotting through the woods.

After, what felt like endless travel, they drew closer to the suburbs of the Sunshine State's subtropical capital. At the sight of many houses on stilts, Sigrid remarked, 'Look, these wooden houses are on posts. They remind me of the prehistoric settlements on the Bodensee. At a glance, they really look similar, except here, the posts don't go into the water.'

Pre-historic settlement

The small identically-sized garden sheds at the end of each backyard were equally puzzling to her, 'Such neat and regimented people live here. They all have the same sized garden sheds. See,' she pointed her arm towards the window 'same, same, and same. Do they also possess the same-sized garden tools?'

'I don't know. It seems odd, though. I never came across anything like that in South Africa,' is all Wolfgang could add.

'Well, to get away from the city, my mother's friend Astrid has a *Schrebergarten* out in the suburbs of Frankfurt. On weekends she loves being in the fresh air of her allotment garden. I've been there a couple of times. But her little hut is bigger than those. These here are just too identical and much too small. How peculiar.'

They did not know that during the mid-1960s, Brisbane was only just in the process of being piped and sewered. The drains could not cope with the regular afternoon showers in summer, and before the 1974 floods, housing lots were regularly inundated. As for the cute little garden sheds, they turned out to be outside toilets, or *dunnies* in the Australian jargon. They were being emptied once a week by a *dunny* man. He came in a truck, carried an empty bin on his shoulder to replace the used one. These were not the only surprises for the couple.

The humidity struck them as they arrived at Brisbane Central Railway Station.

'You can cut this air with a knife. It is like a sauna. I can't breathe.'

'I know, Siggi, it's worse than South Africa. At least there, the heat is dry.'

'Oh, Wolfi, what have we done? I want to go home.'

The thought of having to repay the cost of the journey or any monetary outlay incurred by the Australian Government prompted his retort, 'Let's wait and see.'

They were transported by bus to the Wacol Migrant Hostel. Inauspiciously, the dwellings and fences from those days are today still at the exact location, and the hostel is now renamed Wacol Correctional Centre.

On Sigrid and Wolfgang's arrival, the centre's wooden dwellings were divided into rooms for couples or families, depending on their number. The Schulzes had one room. Another astonishing sight for Sigrid were those weird, corrugated iron huts that were used for accommodation. They looked like upside-down boats. These prompted her reminiscence about her treasured *David Copperfield* book.

How I loved leafing through the pages when I was young. The book belonged to Heinz, a present from his friend Werner. A 1920 German edition. I'd spend hours studying the illustrations by Phiz. Anyway, I'm glad Mother let me have it. That, the photo of Heini with me, and my 'Knusperchen' are the most precious possessions I have in this strange new land.

'Wolfi, in my *David Copperfield* book, such an upside-down boat was a home on the beach. Little Em'ly lived there when Master Davy and Peggotty visited Yarmouth to see her brother. As much as I love that book, I never thought in my wildest dreams that I would follow in Davy's footsteps. Live in an upside-down hut in an upside-down country.'

'Yes, it is odd to live in them today.'

Resembling the setup of a caravan park, a brick building housed an administration block. Another building contained showers, toilets and communal laundry facilities. There was also a child-minding centre. Like any space that accommodates people from different nationalities, the migrants at Wacol followed a uniform routine: set times for three daily meals in the canteen, set times for the weekly pick-up of linen and towels, set times for this, set times for that—set times for living.

Nowadays, these premises accommodate those who have come into conflict with the law and serve their time at her majesty's pleasure. Like the migrants before them, they follow a set routine on their path to reformed integration into society. Somewhat ironically, but to their credit, it seems that Australia cares for both, migrants and prisoners, in the same egalitarian fashion.

Information, hints and gossip were spread during washing sessions at the laundry, 'Did you know Beatrix's family is moving into an apartment in Rosalie?'

'No, really? Where is Rosalie?'

Wolfgang and Sigrid arrived in November, a month that traditionally offered limited employment opportunities for tradesmen, as businesses closed for the Christmas vacation. However, there was a position for a painter in Indonesia. After discussing their options, Wolfgang decided to work there. This left Sigrid alone at the Wacol Hostel.

The closest public transport stops to the camp were either the Wacol or Goodna railway stations. To get there involved a fair amount of walking. Reaching Wacol required a hike through a ruggedly bushy and isolated area. Sigrid took that route quite often, thinking of it as her magic scrubland forest, only realising years later the possible danger associated with her long treks alone to the train station. She also learned the various customs of the land the hard way.

While waiting on the platform after one of her trips into town, another person informed her, 'Lady, there are no trains running. I just found out that there's a strike.'

'Whaaat? How will I get home?'

'Wait till it's over.'

That is totally unheard of in Germany. Unbelievable. What will I do now? I want to go home now, even if it's only an upside-down boat at Wacol.

As Christmas drew closer, someone from the Department of Immigration invited Sigrid for Christmas lunch. A Mr Doyle arrived promptly at twelve o'clock and drove Sigrid to his home in St Lucia, where Mrs Doyle had prepared lunch, sumptuous compared to what Sigrid had been accustomed to since her arrival in Australia. Sigrid never found out how she had been chosen, but she always appreciated the kind-heartedness of her hosts.

On the way back, Mr Doyle showed Sigrid the lusciously green grounds on which The University of Queensland stood. He pointed with pride to the arches, the gargoyles, the great courtyard and the sandstone buildings, exuding an aura of enlightenment. He told Sigrid, 'This is the only university in the state of Queensland.'

This left a lasting impression on Sigrid. She was quite in reverence of the setting and thought with resignation that she would never be able to study there. Would the effect have been as intense had she known what was to happen years later? That is the beauty of life: you never know what it has in store for you. On reflection, one can marvel at the decisions and directions one makes and takes. What seemed too hard and difficult and perhaps unfair, could, in time turn out to be the only way to move forward in life.

The University

After a brief visit from Wolfgang, Sigrid realised she was pregnant. This put an end to her plans of finding work. It was not easy anyway, being stuck out at the hostel.

Wolfgang's contract ran for another twelve months. *No need to rush back for the baby. Life's quite good here. Work's not too bad. Got my mates, got my beer. Better than a screaming kid.*

To prepare for maternity, Sigrid felt it best to move out of the camp into a small flat in the suburb of Rosalie. This was partly caused by remembering her mother's fears about catching spreadable diseases in camps after the war. Moreover, the suburb of Rosalie was relatively close to the hospital, the train, and other amenities. Beatrix Peters, whom Sigrid had already befriended at Wacol, lived there, and provided much support and assistance.

Putting down roots

Encountering real Australians had its droll moments, which Sigrid, with her sense of Teutonic precision, could scarcely accommodate.

Sigrid's neighbour Bev introduced herself, came in for a cup of coffee and then left, 'Ah well, see ya later.' *What did she mean? Is she going to come back this afternoon? Should I wait for her? Maybe she will invite me back to her place?*

It did not take too long for Sigrid to realise that this phrase was just a figure of speech and that the 'later' could, in fact, be quite a while later or even never. The workmen across the road indulged in *smoko*? The *mossies* were biting fiercely. A *cuppa* was offered freely. What is a '*bloke*'? Isn't a man a gent? Could it be a block? Doesn't make sense. A man? But why? *Have a Bex*, it will fix everything. What? What will it fix?

Sigrid had not been taught this colloquialism in her English language classes and had never heard of the need for headache fixing powders. Then there was the habitual 'b' word usually followed by 'hell'! *I hardly know any swearwords in German, 'verdammt'* (damned) *is the worst I can think of.*

Emilie was happy enough to receive the news that she was going to be a grandmother, but her suggestion that Sigrid might want to have the baby in Germany fell on deaf ears. Sigrid felt she had to find her own way in this new country and stand by the decision she made with her husband. *You never know, Wolfi might surprise us with a visit.* Sigrid was correct about the *never*. Wolfgang missed Katrina's birth at the Mater Hospital.

In Sigrid's case, giving birth occurred in a rather unceremonious fashion, not like today when one in twenty-five births are due to an IVF programme associated with careful planning, much anticipation, and exorbitant costs. When Katrina entered this world, the hospital was overcrowded, everybody was rushed off their feet, and the hospital needed additional beds. Sigrid was allocated a folding bed in a sleepout area. Fortunately, Katrina was an easy and quick delivery.

Beatrix visited, holding the newborn, 'What a beautiful baby, such nice white plump skin. Look at those big eyes, dashing hither and thither. You are going to be a clever one, aren't you? Lovely, lovely baby.'

Beatrix assisted the new mother with many considerate tasks. She visited the flat, did some shopping and made sure that Sigrid and her baby daughter could manage.

It was not until November that Wolfgang returned to Australia. By now, the close bond between mother and baby daughter felt exclusionary to him. His weariness was not helped by being in the same situation as when they arrived: the building industry had wound down for the oncoming Christmas season.

He did not take kindly to Sigrid's suggestion, 'Perhaps you could have timed your return more wisely.'

Wolfgang started to drink more heavily. He had always been partial to beer, but now added whiskey to his daily dose. To his credit, Wolfgang was fond of Sigrid and his baby daughter, and there were times when he genuinely tried to make an effort to provide for his little family. But perhaps the unsettling turmoil of his upbringing during the war and the ensuing confusing years of his youth in South Africa made it difficult for him to find his footing in Australia and probably anywhere else for that matter.

In the new year, Wolfgang found odd jobs, but was unable to provide long-term stability and, with that, the foundation to build a permanent nest for his family unit. Days of silence were interrupted by arguments. Moreover, every now and again an apparently unprovoked angry streak surfaced. Periodically, Sigrid also found his behaviour towards her strange and she wondered if he had met another woman. There were times when he came home late, inebriated and animated, or intoxicated and aggressive. His mood swings were unpredictable. He started to gamble and was always short of money. Sigrid had real difficulty managing the household. She became wary of him and his volatile moods.

One day in December was particularly stressful for Sigrid. Katrina was teething and suffering from a cold, leaving very little time for Sigrid to attend to other daily chores or prepare dinner. *I won't have enough money to pay the electricity bill. The car registration is also due. Ah, here he is at last, late, and inebriated.*

'What have you been doing all day? I'm hungry. Where's my dinner? Just so you know, we are not going for camping holidays to Caloundra. I don't have the money. We're going to stay here.'

'But you promised, Wolfgang. I was so looking forward to being on the sea. To get away for once.'

'Yeah, well, shit happens.'

After this quarrel and with Katrina still irritable in her cot, they went to bed.

Exhausted, Sigrid dozed off. She woke to Wolfgang turning over towards her. He started to grunt and rub his erect penis against her left thigh. He then slid his solid body on top of her, ready for penetration. A yawn and sigh escaped from Sigrid's mouth. Wolfgang arched his back briskly and slapped Sigrid across the left side of her cheek with such force that stars appeared in her vision of the darkened room. Feeling guilty, she succumbed yet again to his enforced intercourse. In those days, Sigrid's silent suffering was not an isolated case and only in very recent times has rape in marriage become a punishable offence.

It was years later, in 2011, that Sigrid was to reflect on this traumatic incident after reading an Australian women's magazine that devoted a whole issue to this intolerable situation. She read that, driven by the feminist movement, South Australia was in 1976 at the forefront of reforming laws concerning rape within marriage. Before the 1970s, the foundation of the Australian jurisprudence was based on the seventeenth-century English common law systems. Sir Matthew Hale's articulation was used for this resolution:

[T]he husband cannot be guilty of rape committed by himself upon his lawful wife, for by their mutual matrimonial consent and contract the wife hath given up herself in this kind unto her husband, which she cannot retract.

To Sigrid, it was not surprising that South Australia was the forerunner in seeking social justice for victims of this criminal act since it was also the first Australian state in 1895 to grant women, albeit only those who were British subjects, the right to vote. Sigrid's reading in 2011 also revealed that each Australian state has its own legislation for dealing with sexual offences. Some jurisdictions changed the term marital rape to sexual assault.

On further research on this topic, Sigrid was also to find that an Australian Government resource sheet established that approximately eighty-five percent of sexual assaults never come to the attention of the criminal justice system. Of those reported, only a small percentage result in a successful conviction.

Sigrid's deliberation continued. *Women should not accept physical violation of any kind. But far too many still do. And so did I—back then. Times were just so different. Yet, you still read about this far too often. From an early age it should be instilled in children to always treat each other with respect. If tolerance towards violence is eliminated, society must benefit. I have always instilled that in Katrina. The lack of being respectful is the core issue of violence. Fortunately, Isabella too got that message.*

Fractures

After an argument in their apartment in Rosalie in December 1971, Sigrid complained to Wolfgang that they were not getting anywhere. He grabbed a few of his belongings, jumped into his light-green Holden EK Station Wagon and sped off. It was four days before Christmas and Sigrid had only a few dollars in her purse. She felt utterly and totally trapped and absolutely desperate.

What am I going to do? How can I create some normality during this 'important festive season?' I think I am going out of my mind. She paced up and down the small living room. *How am I going to pay for food? Who could I ask for help? Mother in Germany? But even if I did and admitted Mother's prediction about Wolfgang, there is no way I would get any money before Christmas.*

By now no longer a small baby, Katrina sensed the disharmony and was more niggly than usual. Fortunately, Beatrix called around. She assessed the situation within minutes, bundled Katrina and an unresisting Sigrid into her car, left a note for Wolfgang and drove them to Beatrix's new home in Inala.

Close to neighbouring Wacol, Inala was a housing commission suburb, a government-funded building project for lower-income earners. Most of its residents were migrants, mainly from England. But in Dutch Beatrix's house, filled with three noisy under six-year-olds, Sigrid felt safe and at ease. When Beatrix's husband, the plumber Willem, arrived after work, he did not ask any questions, accepting his wife's decision to extend their hospitality to his wife's friend and her little one.

Sigrid spent that Christmas with the Peterses. It was sad and happy. Sad because of her personal circumstances. She still had no idea where Wolfgang was. Happy because of the kindness with which she was treated by her friends. In those days, the seed was established in her mind: *I will never again be in a situation of dependence; a situation in which I am left almost destitute.* She was unsure how, but she would find work and put Katrina into a kindergarten and create the stability in their lives that Wolfgang could not provide.

Wolfgang reappeared at the beginning of January, somewhat sorry for his behaviour. He had driven to New South Wales, wanting to try his luck in Sydney. He got as far as a caravan park in Coffs Harbour. There he enjoyed bumming around until he ran out of money. His conscience got the better of him, sort of, and he decided to come back to Brisbane, to his wife and daughter.

Sigrid was relieved, and Katrina was happy to see her father again. They all tried to start afresh. Shortly after, on a Saturday morning, just after finishing the morning cleaning routine, Sigrid felt very weak, she was strangely jaundiced, and she instinctively knew she was sick. She lay down on the bed, waiting for Wolfgang to come home. Wolfgang took her to the doctor, who diagnosed, 'Yellow eyes and jaundiced, you've got hepatitis, my dear. You need rest, I can't give you any medication for that. As for you, Wolfgang, I better give you a shot against the inflammation.'

It took more than two months for Sigrid's lethargy to disperse and her energy levels to return. Then one day, she received a telegram from Aunt Rosemarie. Sigrid had expected a letter from her mother, to whom she had conveyed her plans to find a job soon. But her aunt's cable advised Sigrid that her mother Emilie suffered a stroke and had sadly passed away.

Sigrid barely made it to bed. What next? What else could be thrown at her to make her break? It just wasn't fair. Sigrid had planned for her mother to come and visit them in Australia as soon as they had some stability, preferably not while living in the small flat at Rosalie.

Sigrid got up and looked at her mother's photograph in the photo album. She also picked up the wooden-framed photo of her brother Heinz and herself in Schwerin, which seemed many lifetimes ago. If only he had survived the end of the war and hadn't involved himself with some fanatical and misled boys wanting to be heroes. If he were still here, he would help put Wolfgang on the right track. At that moment, Katrina woke from her afternoon nap, 'Mummy, Mummy.'

'My sweet little darling,' Sigrid picked up her child. She cuddled and kissed her and looked deep into Katrina's big blue eyes, 'Mummy will love you forever and promises to look after you. My sweet precious.'

With such an adorable girl, Sigrid had to pull herself together and not succumb to thoughts of melancholy. Once again, Beatrix played a major part in providing moral support to her friend.

Months later, Sigrid received a touching letter with a monetary transfer from Aunt Rosemarie, who had managed Emilie's estate. This boost to their economic situation enabled Sigrid to buy a secondhand Volkswagen Beetle. Around that time, the government offered women who had been out of the workforce due to domestic circumstances the option to gain qualifications at the Kangaroo Point Technical College.

Sigrid grabbed the straw that was offered. It meant that Katrina would have to be cared for. Sigrid found a child-minding centre in Whites Hill. Although out of the way, it was the closest and easiest way to get a placement. The mornings were hardest. Katrina hated going to kindergarten. Every morning she cried, and Sigrid struggled to get her little girl, who did not want to be left at childcare, into the car.

But Sigrid was desperate, this was the only way out of her difficult circumstances. If she got herself a reasonable office job, she'd have the financial independence for which she strove and would never again suffer the consequences of Wolfgang's erratic behaviour. Of course, she loved looking after Katrina, but knew it would be better for her to have one happy parent rather than both being miserable. At least that is what her mother always told Sigrid and she believed it also.

The times Sigrid had spent alone with her mother were wonderful. She thought of that great New Year's Eve in the 1950s in Frankfurt Bornheimer Landstrasse, when they were drinking *Glühwein*, listening to the radio and dancing to the song, *You do have to travel…* That memory always stayed with Sigrid. Indeed, she would have rather wiped-out memories of a number of New Years since her arrival in this new country.

Career growth

For nine months Sigrid maintained the routine of dropping Katrina at day nursery in the morning, driving to Kangaroo Point and learning Business English, Secretarial Practice, Bookkeeping, Shorthand, Typing and Business Machines. She was conscientious and got good results.

One Friday after lunch, Sigrid had a typing class. The teacher Miss Moffatt asked her how many spaces are required after a full stop. Sigrid's mind went blank and suddenly, tears welled up, her breath heaved deep from within her chest, she started sobbing. The eyes of the class were on Sigrid. Miss Moffatt asked what the matter was, and what had upset her. This only made it worse. Miss Moffatt approached Sigrid and led her out of the classroom into the principal's office.

There, both, the principal and deputy principal tried to console Sigrid by asking what had upset her. She could not say and did not know but was still sobbing uncontrollably. After offering her a cup of tea and many tissues, as well as questioning her about how badly she really needed to do this Office Training Course, both ladies suggested it was best for Sigrid to go and see a doctor. Sigrid got herself together as best she could and went to see the doctor at Auchenflower, who asked the same question about her need to do this course. He prescribed Valium.

Sigrid spent that weekend in a daze, but it did not detract from her ambition to find employment. She returned to the college on Monday.

By October 1973, Sigrid had completed all her subjects. She applied for the position of secretary to the accountant of *BAG, Bras and Girdles,* an undergarment manufacturer in Fortitude Valley. To prepare for the interview, Sigrid bought herself a new outfit: a flared green and red floral skirt with a matching bolero jacket, under which she wore a white blouse. Blue block-heeled shoes completed the outfit. Sigrid felt confident.

Of course, she was very nervous when she was called into Mr Moore's office. After a couple of inquiries about her experience (or lack of it), and whether she was pregnant (yes, bosses were then entitled to ask that question), Mr Moore gave Sigrid a notepad and a pen before dictating a letter to her. He then accompanied her to another room and asked Sigrid to type the letter.

With jitters, Sigrid handed Julia, the receptionist, the letter, sat down gingerly and waited in Julia's domain. After what seemed like an eternity, Julia called Sigrid into Mr Moore's office.

'Well, Mrs Schulz, you have made a couple of spelling mistakes, like 'corsetry' and 'brassiere.' However, seeing that these are trade words with which you are obviously not familiar, though you could have done your homework before this interview, well, I'll let it go this once. As our company is in the process of doing negotiations with a German conglomerate, your German language skills are useful to us. Therefore, you are hired on a probationary basis. You can start next Monday. Just close the door behind you if you don't mind.'

Sigrid stood up, stupefied. If she had understood correctly, she had the job. With a timid, 'Yes, thank you,' she opened, walked through, and carefully closed the door.

For some years, Sigrid settled into the routine of working for *BAG* in the Valley. She learned to master the odd stupefying confrontation with English idioms, like typing the minutes of the general meeting when attendees 'move a motion to have matters dropped.' *Why do they all act, as if everything is normal? I only know* that *expression when the doctor asks me about Katrina's bodily functions. Here nobody blinks an eyelid. How weird?*

Katrina had started school and, against Sigrid's trepidations, settled well into school life. The relationship between Sigrid and Wolfgang deteriorated with Sigrid's permanent job.

His drifting now occurred regularly. He went fishing, gambled, drank his beer and was lethargic, meaning—doing nothing. This lack of ambition manifested itself in his inability to keep a job for any length of time. Sigrid increasingly questioned her relationship with Wolfgang. She had had enough. It had been building up for years.

Sigrid sought legal advice to find out how to separate from Wolfgang. The solicitor advised her to live in the same unit for her daughter's sake and because she had no other option, but not to sleep with, cook, or wash for her husband. After one year, she would be able to file for a divorce.

Sigrid told Wolfgang that she wanted a divorce and proposed the new living arrangement to him. He seemed surprised, but it looked as though he accepted the terms. A while later, he questioned her, 'And you will not sleep with me?'

'That's right.' Sigrid went to bed. Dozing off she heard the car starting. *Where is he off to at this hour? Probably the pub! Ah, too tired.*

Still half in slumber, Sigrid was dragged out of bed with inebriated Wolfgang hissing, 'I am going to kill you.' He hauled her through the bedroom and threw her onto the couch in the living room. Sigrid could not fight him off. He sat upon her shoulders and upper torso with all his might, holding her down firmly. He kept punching her again and again on the face, in the eyes, and on the mouth, slurring, 'I am going to destroy you. Your beautiful face. Your eyes. I don't care about your daughter.'

Sigrid could not move. She was breathless, trapped under his colossal body. He kept punching her and saying over and over, 'I'll kill you.'

She expelled a weak gurgling sound, but he kept on punching her. Unable to free herself, her thoughts raced: *This is the end. He is killing me. I am going to die. My daughter, my beautiful girl.*

The blood had splattered everywhere. Wolfgang hesitated and lessened his grip. This allowed Sigrid to escape to the neighbours across the floor.

Bob Mayne called the ambulance. His son Gavin got out his shotgun in case Wolfgang followed. Alarmed, Bob foresaw another tragedy and argued with Gavin about the gun.

The ambulance arrived, the weapon disappeared, and Sigrid was taken to the emergency department at the hospital. Stitches were inserted under her left eye and over her right eye. Sigrid was treated for split lips and lacerations to the face. She was told to see a dentist about the broken front teeth. The staff's sympathy and care became somewhat subdued once they heard that it was 'just another domestic.' They sent her home, where the police were in the process of taking intoxicated Wolfgang away. He was charged with unlawful assault.

The Registrar at the Supreme Court noted the severity of Wolfgang's aggravated assault in the Summons. An injunction was issued to restrain Wolfgang from entering the premises in which Sigrid and her daughter might be residing or from assaulting, threatening, molesting, following, harassing, or otherwise interfering with or contacting Sigrid or her child in any manner whatsoever.

Still, Sigrid was frightened for many months. She feared he would try to carry out his threats again and lived secretly with her child at Inge's home. The psychological scars took many years to heal.

In 1976 counselling was not as widespread as it is today. There were fewer resources. Attitudes often laid the blame on the victim, *she must have asked for it,* thus excusing the perpetrator of domestic violence. At least in the future, a victim of domestic violence could become Australian of the Year, create awareness and work towards building a society that will not tolerate such inhumane behaviour. A society that aspires to respect the dignity of each and every human being.

Sigrid did not anticipate her marriage ending this way. It did, however, inadvertently help her eliminate any kind of sentimental feelings she may have harboured towards Wolfgang before this trauma. As the incident happened during the Christmas festive and merry holiday season, on her return to work in the new year, her bruised eyes had lost their black, blue and red colouring. The stitches were removed, and the umber swelling was only noticeable within close range of her face.

In due course, Sigrid reverted to her birth name Hermes.

A new beginning

Alistair was a contract computer programmer at *BAG*. His desk was situated parallel to Sigrid's, and he too worked closely with Mr Moore. Alistair often told funny jokes to the others working nearby. Sigrid did not really understand them, but everybody laughed, so she joined in. By now, she was used to more Australiana: *cossie* for swimming costume, *having tea* for dinner, *arvo* for afternoon, and she often heard 'bloody' and the occasional 'f' word.

Alistair spent his time setting up procedures for the staff to supply data and use computer programs. He was rather sweet to Sigrid, and she enjoyed his company. They saw each other from time to time, going to the pub on the corner on a Friday after work, or even seeing a play at the SGIO theatre on a Thursday night, when Sigrid could get her neighbour to mind Katrina. By now, it was rather evident that Sigrid and Alistair spent time outside work and colleagues started to talk about them.

One day Mr Moore called Sigrid into his office, 'Close the door and sit down, Sigrid. You are doing a good job here, and your German knowledge is certainly useful. But it has come to the attention of management that you are quite close to Alistair. I must ask you to keep your relationship with him strictly professional. Otherwise, I see no other alternative but to hand you your notice of dismissal. Do you understand what I am saying?'

'Yes, but. Well, alright, Mr Moore.'

This confrontation dumbfounded Sigrid. What had she done? What business of theirs was it with whom she was friends. Another one of those weird Australian rules. She decided not to take too much notice; surely, they could not decide with whom she was allowed to socialise. *And Alistair is such a nice and gentle man. What could they possibly have against him?*

A couple of months after her first reprimand, Mr Moore told Sigrid to come and see him in his office at the beginning of the lunch break. This time he was more serious. 'Sigrid, you have not listened to what I was asking you to do during our last meeting. Now I am really sorry to have to tell you that your work with our company is being terminated. Here is a cheque covering your wages until the end of the month, which is generous on our behalf. Here is a reference for your new employer, which is also complimentary. I must ask you now to pack your belongings and leave our premises. One more thing, your work was always completely satisfactory. You tried hard, and I do wish you the best of luck. I am sorry to have to do this to you.'

Sigrid fought the tears but down they rolled without stopping. Various thoughts raced through her head, but in her emotional state, nothing made much sense. Is that why colleagues talked about joining the union?

To avoid any more drama and further exposing her state of distress, she simply left Mr Moore's office, rummaged through the drawers of her desk, and grabbed her belongings. Since everyone was on lunch, she left the premises, seen only by Julia, the ubiquitous receptionist.

Nothing made sense, Mr Moore was happy with her work, but she was dismissed for seeing Alistair. What did that have to do with her work? How will she manage if she does not get another job? *No, not another horrible pre-Christmas scenario, when I was left without any money.*

The phone started ringing at home. Word spread quickly that Sigrid was gone, and colleagues called to ask what happened. They all seemed genuinely upset at her predicament. Alistair rang and was very quiet after she told him about the dialogue with Mr Moore.

The following morning Sigrid went to the employment office to register and look for work. There might be some casual work with a large department store, but she had to come back the next day. Sigrid aimed to start work as soon as possible.

Unexpectedly, Alistair knocked at her door and threw some light on her unfair dismissal. *BAG* was negotiating a contract with another computer supplier, and Mr Moore was concerned that if Sigrid came across any of the paperwork, she might have imparted this to Alistair. This somewhat eased Sigrid's pain. She knew now that her termination was not an attack on her ability or work skills.

Alistair continued with more news. In five weeks, he was going to work in Canberra on a much bigger project, so *BAG* and Mr Moore could have saved themselves Sigrid's sacking.

He also came up with another piece of positive news, 'You can get any job you like with your skills, Sigrid. For example, there is a new university at Mt Gravatt. They are looking for admin people, and they are full of new ideas and concepts. They are supposed to have good working conditions. Mr Moore would never get away with what he did to you there. I know Mrs Reed, from the secretariat. If you want me to, I'll have a word with her to see if they can use a good worker like you.'

'That would be wonderful, Alistair.'

Alistair spoke with Mrs Reed. Sigrid went for an interview and the job of administrative assistant in the professor's office was hers. Alistair was correct, working at the university was very satisfying. The conditions were better, and there were good opportunities for advancement. Even though Sigrid missed Alistair, who was by now in Canberra, she settled into her new job well. She had no experience with the organisation of universities but quickly grasped the structure of undergraduate and postgraduate degrees, subject outlines, assessments and the correct lettering of PhD, whose ostensibly esoteric concept was to become a theme of personal significance.

One day Professor Morris, the head of the Centre for the Advancement of Learning and Teaching, gave Sigrid some handwritten notes to type for a presentation to graduating Year Twelve students. He congratulated them on their achievement of completing high school, emphasising that this was only the beginning of their journey in their quest for knowledge. 'Learning is a lifelong process.' This really struck a chord with Sigrid. She felt inspired.

The university had a generous staff incentive scheme that supported its employees to further their education. A number of mature-age women in the university were undertaking studies through this scheme. Feeling encouraged and remembering her reverence for the only university on her first Christmas in Australia, when generous Mr Doyle had driven her around its grounds, she decided to post an application. Sigrid was accepted and enrolled in a Bachelor of Arts majoring in English and German. The wonderful feeling of walking on those esteemed university grounds did not dissipate on her first day.

A surprise visit from Aunt Rosemarie brought Sigrid immense happiness. Still robust, Rosemarie, having lost her partner in Germany, decided to visit the other side of the globe. 'I have to see my *little* niece again and meet my grand-niece Katrina, while I still can.' There was much to catch up. Sigrid took Rosemarie to tourist spots like Lone Pine Koala Sanctuary. They spent a weekend on the Sunshine Coast, where Rosemarie decided to stay for the week. Sigrid together with Katrina surprised Rosemarie with tickets to the performance of 'Giselle' at the

Queensland Ballet. Back at the flat, they reminiscent about the times spent in Schwerin during the war. Katrina pored over the faded photograph of Rosemarie as a young dancer in Germany, causing all three to wipe tears from their eyes.

Rosemarie's dance

The weekend before Rosemarie's return flight to Frankfurt, Sigrid had an invite to a party at Benson Street, Toowong. Rosemarie was also welcome; she was keen to meet real Australians. And she did. While everybody, being generally young, was gyrating to the latest groove, Rosemarie sat in a corner sipping on a glass of white wine. The host Russell, observing the still classy lady, gallantly bent down and asked the German guest for a dance. Their dancing was beautiful to watch, and it was most touching to read Rosemarie's thoughts, 'This is probably the last time anybody is going to ask me for a dance.' And it was. She left Australia with very happy memories.

Sigrid studied for six years part-time at night, doing two subjects per semester. She was disciplined and used weekends and free evenings to research. In doing this, Sigrid set a good example for Katrina, who also became studious. Her school progress benefitted.

By the time Sigrid received her Bachelor of Arts, she had decided to become a high school teacher. After a quiet celebratory dinner with Katrina and Alistair, she enrolled in a Graduate Diploma in Education. During the next two years, she often experienced a sense of deep achievement and satisfaction walking in the hallowed grounds of her sandstone university.

On gaining her Graduate Diploma, Sigrid and Katrina went out for dinner to *Angelo's*, an Italian restaurant in Toowong to celebrate their respective successes. Katrina commenced an Environmental Studies degree at university.

Sigrid had an offer to teach at Gympie. As Katrina found student accommodation on campus, they put their furniture into storage and left, not without an emotional farewell from Beatrix, Sigrid's first friend in Australia.

Sigrid spent four years in Gympie. She enjoyed teaching, and as a qualified native speaker, her German language skill was in demand.

Katrina completed her studies, which mother and daughter celebrated with other graduands after her award ceremony. Katrina found employment with the Parks and Wildlife Organisation and Sigrid had finished her country service and was now teaching at Coorparoo.

The years went by. Katrina met Peter and they married in the late 1990s. Sigrid taught at Kenmore and bought a cottage there. Alistair had resurfaced from Canberra, and Katrina saw that Sigrid spent many happy hours with him.

The message of lifelong learning instigated by Professor Morris prompted Sigrid to apply for enrolment in a PhD. Her proposed thesis topic about the emancipatory endeavours of female German writers in the mid-nineteenth century was accepted. She was inspired by Ida von Hahn-Hahn's daring suggestion in 1834 to send boys to sewing schools and girls to universities to see how different society would be after three generations: an extraordinary proposal, even in present times.

For five years, Sigrid researched and worked long hours. At times when she complained and felt unable to cope, trusty Alistair's, 'just keep writing,' spurred her forward. She presented papers at graduate conferences in other capital cities and New Zealand. Her university grant allowed her to research primary sources and meet scholars in Germany. Wearing her floppy hat to receive her PhD was her apotheosis. She pondered with tears how she, the migrant who arrived with nothing but youth, naivety, no great expectations and only her treasured photograph of Heinz, her linden timbered *Knusperchen* and *David Copperfield*, was now receiving her doctorate from the Chancellor of *the* University many years after she first set foot on this continent.

This conferral led to her lecturing at university. She relished the interaction with her students. Sigrid was in her element imparting the rules of grammar and being immersed in her native language. She always felt invigorated after lively discussions about the culture and traditions of her home country and shared with her students their excitement of a burgeoning career or a forthcoming trip to Germany.

It also led to Sigrid working occasionally at the state art gallery, where she translated intertitles for silent movies and subtitles for movies with sound. During the screenings of those German films, she performed keyboard functions. A hair-raising exercise, when a slow or hesitant pressing of the key results in subtitles being out of sync with the movie's dialogue. But Sigrid loved all the films with which she worked, from FW Murnau of the 1920s, to Martin Walz's 1996 horror comedy *Killer Condom*.

When Katrina gave birth to Isabella, Sigrid was there to support her daughter. She held her granddaughter and was filled with an enormous feeling of affection. 'You beautiful baby. I am going to be a good oma for you. And I will spoil you. Why?' Sigrid caressed Isabella's cheeks, 'Because I can. Yes, I can. In a few years when you are older, I will take my nicely dressed up granddaughter to cafés, to the *Nutcracker* ballet at Christmas time, to *Peter and the Wolf*, and to the children's activities at the Gallery of Modern Art. I will, I will, oh, yes, I will... You beautiful baby.'

Retiring from her teaching at university, Sigrid anticipated more involvement with her grandchild. Alas, she only had a few years for all the planned outings with her little darling, as Katrina and Peter moved to Gladstone in 2007. Sigrid understood that Peter felt he had a huge responsibility in his new job. With the company workforce amounting to almost two thousand employees, he had to maintain safe workplace conditions and ensure a reduction in injury and environmental incidents. Sigrid heard all about his prevention of 'any incidents.' How he constantly applied 'his three-step: training, inspecting and reviewing.' How he 'knew that to maintain the company's excellent reputation, not only in Gladstone but around the world, he had to do all he could to stay ahead of the pack.' Yes, Sigrid understood all this extremely well.

Now she enjoyed the occasional visits of her fast-growing granddaughter, only occasionally indulging in her fantasies about proposed precious times together.

8. Australia 2013

Fundraiser

Hugo, the coveted caterer, announced his arrival on the intercom at Rose's ground floor entrance at five o'clock sharp on Saturday, the fifth of October. He appeared at the penthouse door, where Rose was introduced to his assistant, Gloria, and the waiters. Keeping their eyes on Hugo's polished bald spot, the staff followed his determined short steps as they strategically positioned boxes and cartons in Rose's kitchen.

Fascinated, Rose watched the magic unfold. An arrangement of sparkling champagne flutes, rounded tumblers, wine glasses, water glasses, side plates, dinner plates, dessert plates, cups with saucers, cutlery, napkins, and stunning floral displays of scented white and pink lilies, was all organised in an orderly fashion. The food and drinks remained concealed in neat stackable cartons.

'Hugo, just as I had expected, it's shaping up splendidly, sweetie.'

'Thanks, darling. Of course, I handpicked the crème de la crème of staff and as usual, I personally supervised the sourcing of all ingredients and merchandise.'

'Quite, quite. Here is a list of guests for Gloria. I'll leave you to it.'

Rose disappeared into the inner sanctum of her sumptuous apartment.

David was the first to be greeted by Gloria at six o'clock. He was followed by Eva and Werner. David was glad that Werner was one of the first invitees to arrive.

'Hello Eva, hello Werner. How are you?'

'Well, thanks, David. It's good to see you,' answered Werner.

Other *Apricity* committee members and guests seemed to pour in all at once. As quickly as the arriving guests lifted the champagne flutes, the drinks were replenished by the waiters.

'It's nice to see you, David. Please excuse me. I must pass something to our Chair. Ah, Roger's over there.' Eva turned and disappeared in the mingling crowd.

Sigrid arrived with Katrina, Peter and Isabella. Before crossing the threshold of Rose's door, Katrina uttered in a conspiratorial *sotto voce*, 'Mother, are you sure we should have come with you?'

'Of course, dear. We don't have to stay long. Just have a glass of bubbly,' Sigrid whispered under her breath and with a smile.

'Good evening. I am Gloria. Can I have your names please?'

'Sigrid Hermes, with Peter, Katrina and Isabella Wallace.'

'Please, do help yourselves to some refreshments,' Gloria beckoned to the closest drink waiter.

Roger's stentorian voice endorsed Rose's appearance, 'Ooh, here she is.'

The volume of the general babble lowered. An overall 'good evening', 'hi' and 'hello' tapered off with Rose's 'Welcome, darlings. I am happy to see so many of you here tonight. Here is a toast to a successful fundraiser for *Apricity*.' Rose raised her glass, a gesture followed by the guests whose babble resumed promptly.

Over the sea of heads, Sigrid spotted David, 'Come, let me introduce you to my friend,' Sigrid hooked into Katrina's arm, steering towards David's direction. Peter and Isabella followed. Finally, Katrina would be able to set eyes on the mysterious David.

'Hello, David. Meet my daughter Katrina, my son-in-law Peter, and my granddaughter Isabella.'

'Well, well. How nice to see you, Sigrid. And I am very pleased to meet you, Katrina, Peter, and Isabella. Sigrid often talks about you.' He turned towards Werner, 'Sigrid, I'm not sure if you and Werner have met? Let me introduce you.'

By now, Eva had returned and joined the group. Somehow the dynamics of the groups segregated into male and female circles, as happens so often at social gatherings. In response to Eva's admiration of Katrina's ring with the blue pearl, Katrina was telling her story of finding the little shop at Hervey Bay. The talk of gorgeous jewellery prompted Isabella to describe the ancient and exquisitely worked pieces, particularly the golden belt buckle, that she had seen and sketched at the museum's *Hidden Treasure* exhibition. The other females agreed that they should definitely make an effort to see it.

Meanwhile, Rose dragged David over to talk to Roger. Werner and Peter found a connection and moved onto the balcony. They discussed occupational health and safety standards. The conversation turned from the use of nail guns in public places to workplace efficiency. Then Werner remembered one of the world's first transistorised computers used in 1960 for six years.

'It was called SNOCOM, and its purpose was to speed up the whole process of the Snowy Hydro Scheme.'

'I know, that is really interesting. I've seen the SNOCOM computer at the National Museum in Canberra,' Peter responded.

Looking to the east over the dark firmament contrasting the high-lighted city skyline with its gyrating reflection in the river, Peter held his arms out and traced a square with his finger saying, 'That would make a great shot.'

'Are you into photography?' Werner quizzed.

'It's a hobby,' Peter responded. 'It is amazing what you can do with digital photography these days. Mind you, some of the most wonderful photographs are in black and white. I am thinking of Helmut Newton's tantalising portraits and also the stark and unexpected effects of negative imaging of Man Ray's photograms or rayographs as he liked to call them.'

'Yes, back in my youth, we used the good old Brownie to take black and white snapshots. We then developed them ourselves.'

'Ah, really. Brownie Six-20? What a coincidence. I've brought a genuine vintage Brownie Six-20 with me from Gladstone. It is one of the early ones, made in Germany before the war. It's for my nephew's birthday. I'm dropping it off tomorrow before heading home.'

'You don't say. An actual Brownie?'

'Yes, I bought it over the net. I can show it to you, if you like. We are staying with my mother-in-law till tomorrow afternoon. I'm sure she won't mind if you come over before then.'

Werner became more and more interested, 'Well, I wouldn't mind seeing and touching an old Brownie again. Why not? Let's see Sigrid and find out if it suits and then organise a time.'

Peter and Werner located Sigrid between the guests, who were by now enjoying the petit fours and coffee. In between nibbling and sipping, the arrangement was made for Werner to drop by Sigrid's place before two o'clock the next day. Judging by the animation, laughter, humour and overall buzz in the penthouse, donations flowed generously. A good time was had by all, including Katrina, whose garnered scrutiny of David had abated after observing the reassuring demeanour during his social interactions.

A little while later, one by one Rose's guests bid their farewell until David was the only one left. While Hugo gave some last cleaning instructions to his staff, Rose asked, 'A nightcap before you go, David sweets?'

'How can I say no! When you ask, it's not a question. It's a command, my dear.'

'That is my prerogative, and let's keep it that way. A Drambuie?'

'As smooth as your tongue. Why not!'

'Why not, indeed. I believe tonight went well?'

'Yes, like anything you organise, dear.'

'You dear *charmeur,* I believe you, just this once.' Rose raised her glass to David's.

Revelation

After a leisurely breakfast of eggs and spinach on sourdough for Sigrid, Katrina and Peter, and Bircher Muesli with yoghurt and strawberries for Isabella, the three generations of females sat around the pool. At the same time Peter offered, and was not dissuaded, to clear away the breakfast dishes.

'If you were not going to Germany in winter, I'd suggest that you take a train to Heiligendamm on the East coast. But then, I, as your oma, should really come with you and show it to you.'

'Let's keep that in mind. Perhaps Oma could take you there on her next trip to Germany. What do you think, Bella?' Turning to Sigrid, Katrina continued, 'But, maybe we should wait and see how she likes Germany first. Don't you think, Mutti?'

'Yes, of course, she'll like it. You mark my word. She'll love it.'

'I might just go and see how Dad is getting on.' Isabella got up and ambled towards the house.

'Why are you always so impulsive, Mother? Take one step at a time. It will all work out.'

'Oh yes, I know, I just got a bit excited. I didn't mean to jump ahead. What about you? Have you got any plans to travel?'

Katrina pressed her lips together, shrugged and moved her hands outwards.

Sigrid regretted that she had got ahead of herself again, *verdammt, that's now the second time I did it within minutes.* She knew she must be more measured in the way she approached matters. Years of teaching had not curbed her unguarded impulses, while irksome to Katrina, agreeable to her students. Yet, she found the social restraints to be stronger in Australia than in Germany. While Australians strive to project the image of a free nation, on a personal level, they seem to be more inhibited than Germans. This observation manifested itself only in recent times, after starting her trips to the country of her birth. She did not really know any Germans in the Western suburbs. Meeting Eva's husband, Werner made that an exception. Though, to Sigrid, he was rather reserved. *Of course, he had already spent many years in Australia.*

Peter flopped down along the edge of the pool. Isabella played with Schatzi, the Dachsie, and Katrina was reading the morning paper. Each enjoyed the quiet, interspersed with the occasional rustle of the wind through the surrounding trees and the intermittent sibilant birds busily gossiping.

After a light lunch, Werner arrived just as Peter was loading the car with the overnight bags and Isabella's colourful suitcase.

'Hi, your timing is excellent. Come on in.' The two men shook hands.

'Hello. I couldn't let an opportunity like this slip past. The last time I held a Brownie was in 1944. A long time ago.'

Peter guided Werner through the entrance into the open living and dining area where his nephew Max's present stood unwrapped on the dining table. Lifting the Brownie out of the box, Peter placed it in Werner's hands. Werner tenderly ran his fingers along the edges and the lens aperture settings. He held the box down near his waist and looked through the view finder. Werner then continued to examine the control information that still showed the lettering: *Landschaft* (landscape) on top of *Gruppe* and *Porträt*.

'Holding this little box brings back memories, fond memories, and sad memories that I have tried to forget. Tried to obliterate from my life, really.'

Peter remained quiet.

After a pause, Werner added, 'Thank you so much for allowing me to get in touch with some of my old self.' Werner handed the Brownie back to Peter.

'Well, hello. Welcome to my home,' Sigrid broke the moment of silence. She extended her right hand to Werner. 'Would you like a cold drink?'

'No thanks, dear. You do have a very nice place, Sigrid. It's tranquil, and I like your books everywhere. You have quite a bit of reading there.'

'Yes, at this stage of my life, I have the time to read and enjoy it too.' Sigrid replied.

'Hello, Werner,' said Katrina.

'Hello, Dr Mueller,' said Isabella, entering through the hallway.

'You are all packed and ready for your drive back to Gladstone. I won't intrude on you any longer.'

Werner turned towards the entrance when, as if electrified, he swung around and positioned himself right in front of the bookcase with the framed photograph showing Sigrid and Heinz. He picked up the frame and scrutinised the photo.

'Where was this taken?' he asked. 'When was this taken?' he continued shrilly.

'In Schwerin. In 1944. Why?' Sigrid answered, slightly agitated in response to Werner's harsh line of questioning. Her curiosity was on high alert. The others stood spellbound.

'Is this your brother?' Werner questioned, pointing to Heinz in the photo.

'Yes, that was my brother. Heinz,' Sigrid answered awkwardly.

Uninvited, Werner sat down in the armchair with the photo frame in both hands. He turned pale and his hands were shaking. Silently observing the scenario, Peter put a glass of water on the side table next to Werner. As if in a trance, Werner put the carved frame into his lap and picked up the glass, wetting his lips.

The carefree atmosphere was now charged with silent tension.

Werner straightened his back and looked up into Sigrid's eyes.

'Sigrid, please, do sit down. I have to confess something to you.'

'We better leave you to it,' Peter said, putting his arms around Katrina and Isabella.

'No, there is no need. What I have to say, needs to be said, and sooner or later you will find out about it. It is best you hear it from me now,' Werner responded. After a deep breath, he added, 'You all better sit down.'

Katrina and Isabella sat on the couch. Peter remained standing.

Lifting the photo frame from his lap Werner, with tears in his eyes, his hand trembling more and his quiet yet rasping voice, continued, 'Sigrid, in 1944 your brother Heinz and I became very good friends. We were both grouped into the same Hitler Youth camp in Malchin. We both liked outdoor activities as well as taking snapshots. Yes, I had my Brownie Six-20, but Heinz had an Agfa Synchro. Heinz was different to other boys. He had integrity, he was considerate, and he used his brain to think.'

Werner paused and took another sip of water. Audibly inhaling, he continued gravelly, 'Because Heinz thought with intelligence and virtue, he saw what I did not. He understood what I did not. He died, and I did not.'

At this point, Werner could no longer restrain his emotions. Sobbing, his hands shaking, he put down the photo frame on the side table and buried his face in his hands.

In disbelief and wonderment, the others stared at this seemingly dignified man, this man whom they only met the night before, and who now exposed his innermost feelings in front of them. Sigrid moved in her chair anxiously. Peter, ready to take whatever action might be needed, kept a calm eye on the whole situation.

Werner pulled himself together. 'My dear Sigrid, you were only small when your brother was shot in 1945. Your mother would have received one version of how he died. But sadly, I need to disclose the tragic truth surrounding the circumstances of his death. I have carried this burden for far too long.'

'Is that really necessary?' Peter interjected.

'Yes, I need to know.' Sigrid whispered.

Peter handed Sigrid a glass of water.

Werner continued, 'Sigrid, the account of Heinz's death was that he was involved in throwing a hand grenade onto the first of the oncoming British tanks. An English soldier responded by shooting him.'

'Yes, I heard something like that,' Sigrid replied.

Werner took a deep breath, 'It was me who tried to throw the hand grenade.'

'What? Who? You? After all these years? What do you mean?'

Sigrid could not think straight. This was unexpected. It was too overwhelming.

'It was me who tried to throw the grenade. I should have been the one who died. Your brother tried to wrestle the weapon out of my hand, and in the kafuffle, a bullet killed him instead of me. I have regretted this all my life. Your brother was innocent of all that was happening in those terrible years. He was only fourteen, only one year older than me, but he was wise and considerate.'

Sigrid sat in stony silence.

Werner continued, 'I told them the truth. They were all around me. Boys, civilians, the Brits, the teacher. I never forgot his name. Herr Rindermann. I guess he felt sorry for me and wanted to give me a fresh start. But I did not ask for that, nor did I want it. His decision of inaction has haunted me all my life. I wanted to be punished. I begged to be punished. There was no point in my lying. Heinz was the best friend I ever had.

I wrote a letter to your mother. I rode a bike from Hamburg to Frankfurt. I waited anxiously outside your apartment block. You came around the corner. When I heard a commanding voice from the opened window yelling at me to get lost, I panicked. I asked if you were Siggi. I gave you the letter and fled. I know I shouldn't have. You were still so young. But I panicked and ran away. Heinz's death has haunted me. I have had to live with it. I am still living with it.'

Sigrid heard all she could take. She got up and left the room. Katrina followed her mother. Isabella followed both.

In acknowledging Werner's tumultuous ordeal, Peter poured Werner a *Jägermeister*. When Werner calmed down, Peter saw him to the door.

Once Sigrid was more composed, both Katrina and Isabella wanted to stay with their mother and grandmother. But Sigrid felt she needed to be on her own. She promised to fly to Gladstone sooner rather than later. Feeling certain there was nothing more they could do for the moment; Sigrid's family somberly commenced their journey home.

Sigrid made herself a cup of tea. She sat in her rocking chair facing the view of the palm trees outside.

It wasn't Heinz. It was Werner. Now I am beginning to understand how Mother felt. It was so out of character for Heinz to throw the grenade. Mother always said so. How I wish she would have had this confirmed while she was still alive.

Sigrid vaguely remembered the strange incident in Lilliencronstrasse of an unfamiliar boy, with an abrupt manner, pushing something into her hand. She recalled the enjoyment of playing chasey and hopscotch with the kids across the street until her mother came home. However, she didn't remember a letter. Or did she? Had she lost it? Forgotten it? If only she'd been aware of its importance. If only she had.

Sigrid reflected on what she remembered of her brother. The last two days in Schwerin. Her birthday. The squirrel he carved for her. The boat excursion to the castle the following day. She thought of his kindness, the way he looked after her, protected her, the way she saw aspects of Heinz's character in Wolfgang when she first met him with Sonia in Frankfurt. She pondered how different life would have been for her and Mother if Heinz had lived.

Now, sixty-eight years later, Sigrid finds that the person who was responsible for Heinz's death is not only living here in Australia but almost in the next suburb. How could Werner live with the consequences of his behaviour and involvement in Heinz's death?

Indeed, how could Werner live with his revelation to Sigrid and her family?

Finally, at just over eighty years of age, Werner had unloaded what had been such a heavy burden all his life. Back at his home in The Gap, he picked up the photo they had taken on the Remplin staircase in 1944 and sat down in his swivel chair.

Werner thought about the *best* day, when both boys cycled to the observatory, how they sat on the upper platform, at peace and happy with the world at that moment. An Elie Wiesel quote he had heard in a television interview a while ago came to his mind: 'To stand by silent and indifferent, is the greatest sin of all.'

Had Werner stood by silent and indifferent? Searching within the depths of his heart and upon further contemplation, Werner concluded that he was not guilty of that sin. He had not been silent. He told the truth to Herr Rindermann. He told his Uncle Otto. He wrote a letter to Frau Hermes. He told Sigrid; he chose to speak out. And he certainly had never been indifferent about what happened. He chose the harder path of studying while working. He chose to serve his fellow human beings in the best humanitarian way he was capable. He had, and always would honour Heinz's memory. Being able to convey to Sigrid the truth about Heinz's death was a cathartic experience for Werner, who now felt at peace enough to leave this world, whenever that would be.

Epilogue

After some weeks, during which Sigrid spent much time in deliberation, Werner received a short note:

Monday, 4 November

Dear Werner

I now understand the real and sad circumstances that led to Heinz's tragic death. And, I realise how difficult it must have made your life, living with that memory.

Although I was only seven years old when this happened, I do remember the hard times before and after the war. I am also aware of the fanatical indoctrination of the Nazi regime. Hardly anyone escaped its consequences unscathed. I also recall a boy giving me a piece of paper for my mother. This was obviously you. If only I had been more careful, I would not have lost it, and we would have had answers years ago.

Growing up I often leafed through the 'David Copperfield' book. I read it several times and always wondered about the Werner *dedication.*

After much contemplation, I have concluded that were Heinz still alive, he would want us to be friends. Because Heinz was such a special person, there is much love associated with his personality. I loved him in my way, and you loved him in yours. Our love of Heinz unites us.

I would like to invite you and Eva for afternoon coffee on my return from Gladstone after the fifteenth of November.

Please give me a ring and we will set a date.

Kind regards
Sigrid

Glossary

Abbr	German	English
DJV	Deutsches Jungvolk	young people of Germany
HJ	Hitlerjugend	Hitler Youth
HJS	Hitler Jugend Signal	Hitler Youth signal training
JB	Jungbann	German Youth folk unit
JSF	Jungenschaftsführer	group leader for the under 15-year-old HJ
KLV	Kinderlandverschickung	Government regulated dispatch of children to the country
NSDAP	Nationalsozialistische Deutsche Arbeiterpartei	National Socialist German Workers' Party
NS	Nationalsozialistisch	national socialist
NSVW	NS-Volkswohlfahrt	NS People's welfare
Pf	Pimpf	cub-after 1933 10-14-year-old boys of HJ
RJF	Reichsjugendführung	Youth Realm Directorate
RHS	Reichs Hauptschule	secondary school
VS	Volkssturm	territorial army raised at the end of WWII

List of Works Consulted

Australian Government Resource Sheet. Australian Government, Australian Institute of Family Studies, Australian Centre for the Study of Sexual Assault, Sexual assault laws in Australia, ACSSA Resource Sheet.

Bock, Sabine. *Schwerin Die Altstadt. Stadtplanung und Hausbestand im 20. Jahrhundert.* Schwerin: Helms, 1996.

Dahlenburg, Geoffrey W. *Medical education in Australia: changes are needed. It is time for less talk and more action.* MJA Vol. 184. 319–320.

Die Brücke. Directed by Bernhard Wicki. Performed by Volker Lechtenbrink et al., Fono-Film GmbH (Berlin), 1959.

Geffen, Laurence. *A brief history of medical education and training in Australia.* MJA Vol. 201. 519–520.

German prisoners of war in the Soviet Union. https://en.wikipedia.org/wiki/German_prisoners_of_war_in_ the_Soviet_Union

Hale, Sir Matthew as quoted in P Easteal and C Feerick, *Sexual Assault by Male Partners: Is the Licence Still Valid?* (2005) Flinders Journal of Law Reform Vol. 8. No. 2. 185, 186.

Heine, Heinrich, *Ludwig Börne*, Eine Denkschrift. Zweites Buch (1840), (Brief aus Helgoland vom 1. Juli 1830).

Lange, Wilhelm. *Cap Arcona.* Neustadt: Sparkassen-Kulturstiftung Ostholstein, 2014.

McGoldrick, Kirsty. *Snowfraus. The Women of the Snowy Mountain Scheme.* Sydney: Kangaroo Press, 1998.

McHugh, Siobhán. *The Snowy, a history*. Sydney: NewSouth Publishing, 2019.

National Archives of Australia. International Refugee Organisation-Australian Government agreement https://www.naa.gov.au/learn/learning-resources/learning-resource-themes/society-and-culture/migration-and-multiculturalism/international-refugee-organisation-australian-government-agreement

Nippoldt, Robert, and Boris Pofalla. *Night Falls on the Berlin of the Roaring Twenties*. Cologne: Taschen, 2018.

Stiftung Topographie des Terrors. *Deutschland 1945 – Die letzten Kriegsmonate*. Berlin: Conrad Citydruck, 2014.

The New Order by the Editors of Time-Life Books. Time-Life, Alexandria, Virginia, 1990.

Witzleben, Siegmar. *Kriegsende und Neubeginn in Ostholstein 1945. Zeitzeugen berichten aus dem "Kral"*. Oldenburg: GloeSS, 2005.

Acknowledgements

A heartful thanks to my wonderful editors, friends, writers' group members, and family, without whom this book would not be what it is.

Thank you, Gary Crew, Emeritus Professor, I have learned and benefitted from your vital structural advice and edits. Donna Munro, your numerous edits, priceless suggestions and skilled support made this publishing journey possible. Katalin Gaal, your revision and reassurance gave me the courage to persevere. Linda Stewart, for your valuable edit in the final stage.

Thank you, Eva Turek-Jewkes, for your support and initial structural feedback. Deborah Eddy for suggestions and reassurance.

Thank you, Professor Cliff Rosendahl, for sharing medical training information and encouragement.

Thank you, Mark for explaining Workplace Health and Safety procedures. Aisha and Marlee for sharing a young person's point of view.

Thank you, Martin Knox, for pointing me into the right publishing direction. Nancy Cox-Milliner of the Writers of Seville and Kelly Lyonns of the Ashgrove Writing Group together with fellow writers from these groups for the encouragement, friendship, and camaraderie.

Thank you, Chris Grace from the Queensland Writers Centre for much appreciated feedback.

Thank you, Geoff Ginn, for your sketch of Heinz and Sigrid.

Thank you, Ildika and Kate for your support.

A very special thank you to Geoff for your inestimable encouragement, editing, patience, belief in me and my ability to *just keep writing*.

Thank you, dear reader, for sharing the journey of Heinz, Sigrid and Werner.

Finally, no, I am not on the *Jägermeister* payroll.

CPSIA information can be obtained
at www.ICGtesting.com
Printed in the USA
LVHW101936100622
720908LV00003B/33